ALONE IN MIAMI AT 3AM 3

J. DOMINIQUE

Alone In Miami At 3AM 3

Mailing List

To stay up to date on new releases, plus get information on contests, sneak peeks, and more,

Go To The Website Below...

www.coleheartsignature.com

ZURI

My body immediately stiffened, seeing my sister standing there. I still had yet to deal with my feelings when it came to her, and I couldn't help looking at my father funny for ambushing me. I didn't even know how to act. Should I force a smile? Hug her? The truth was, even if I genuinely tried to get along with her, it probably wouldn't be well received, especially after she'd just lost her baby. My face twitched as I tried to get my bearings.

"Hey, Daddy. Hey, Kendra," I mustered up while Shai, on the other hand, remained silent. She didn't seem to be expecting that, and she turned up her nose as my daddy pulled a chair out for her.

"Really, Kadeem?" My mama, who'd been shooting daggers at him, finally spoke once he pulled his own chair up to the table.

He seemed surprised by her question and shrugged like he hadn't done anything wrong. "Really what, Zora? You over there mugging me like I did something to you."

"Fool, you know exactly what I'm talking about. Don't play with me! Why would you bring this damn girl here, knowing—"

"I thought it was a family dinner! Ain't she family?"

"Hey, hey, y'all calm down. It's really not a big deal, Ma." I tried to squash it before things got any more out of hand. They were already yelling at someone else's dinner table, and this was only our

first time meeting. My cheeks burned with embarrassment, and I avoided eye contact with everyone at the table.

"Hell naw, 'cause he's really showin' his ass tonight!"

"Look, I don't know what your problem is with me, lady, but your daughter got pregnant by my man, not the other way around." Kendra's face held a look of satisfaction like she'd been ready to unload that clip for months.

"The man you cheated on? Little girl, I'm trying not to take it there with you, but on my dead mama—" Queen was at the end of the table, already trying to take off her earrings. I looked around to see if anybody was going to stop her, but no one moved a muscle.

My mama waved her off with a snort, and I dropped my head in my hand and blew out a deep breath. "I could give a fuck less about who got pregnant first. My only concern is my grandson, and I'm not about to let you put him at risk for this petty shit!" My mama's words had so much bite to them that I damn near saw smoke coming out of her ears.

She turned to Shai, who was still silently eating like nothing was going on, and I knew she was about to get crazy from the look in her eye.

"So, you're having a son? Are you making him a junior like we discussed?"

"This bitch crazy," Zaakir grunted, shaking his head. "You want me to throw her out, Queen?"

"I got it." Shai's voice was dangerously calm as he pushed away from the table. He made it to the other side fast as hell and snatched her out of the chair she was sitting in.

"Hey—" my dad tried to interject.

"Nigga, you can go too"! Zaakir stood and lifted his shirt to show the butt of a gun I hadn't noticed this whole time.

My dad's mouth instantly snapped shut, and he threw his hands defensively in front of him.

"Everybody calm down." Giorgio stood next, speaking in a calm tone.

By then, Kendra was struggling with Shai as he tried to drag *her away from the table, so nobody noticed Queen coming. All I saw was a flash of navy blue, and she was on top of Kendra, throwing the fastest barrage of punches I'd ever seen. Chaos ensued, and while Zaakir was cheering her on, his father was still eating like this was an everyday occurrence. Giorgio and Shai attempted to pull Queen away from a now bloodied Kendra, and my dad just looked like he didn't know what to do.*

"Bitch, I been wanting to beat yo' ass! I told you!" Queen shouted as Giorgio finally lifted her off the girl and dragged her kicking and screaming into the kitchen while Shai ran a stressed hand across his head.

"You people are fuckin' crazy!" my dad exclaimed, dropping to check on Kendra.

"And you're a shit starter! Fuck would make you bring her here? Zuri's pregnancy is already high risk, and every time I turn around, you're throwing this bitch in her face when you know the situation! Look at what you did!" Shai pointed my way, and I didn't understand what he was talking about until I felt a tear land on my hand.

"This is her sister! Her family! That's my job to make sure they have a relationship!" my dad argued as he finally lifted a staggering Kendra to her feet, and I gasped. Queen had really fucked her up, but I didn't know if I should feel bad for her or not. She'd really brought that ass whooping on herself by poking the bear. "Zuri, is this the type of people you want to raise my grandson around? Pulling out guns and attacking your sister!" His face was balled up in disgust as he looked around the room.

"I think you need to leave right now, Kadeem," my mama managed to get out.

I could tell she was just as horrified as he was, but she was also too angry at him to address anything else. Or maybe she just didn't want to further upset me.

"Yeah, you're stepping into dangerous territory. Head on out." Casa never stopped eating as he sent a warning before giving my father a threatening glare. My dad eventually stormed out,

mumbling under his breath. Casa casually looked across the table at me and my mama with a charming grin. "Sorry, but he was trippin'." He shrugged.

"This nigga." Zaakir chortled, already back in his chair.

"I think I should get you home. Just let me check on my OG right quick," Shai said lowly before swiftly disappearing into the kitchen where his father had taken his mama.

Once he was gone, the only sounds that could be heard were Zaakir and Casa's forks scraping the bottom of their plates as they continued eating. I was literally too stunned to react, too stunned to move, and confused as hell. That whole scene had escalated quick as hell, and everyone in Shai's family had an insane reaction to the mess.

"Zuri! Are you okay?" My mama squeezed my arm with her brows drawn in concern. "I been calling you. Are you alright?" she repeated, wiping the tears from my cheeks.

I still didn't know how to answer that because a mix of emotions was swirling around inside me.

"I'm..." I searched for the right words, eyes darting around as if they would jump off the table and into my mouth. "I'm fine—"

"Zuri, baby, let's go." Shai came back, cutting me off before I could get to lying.

I was anything but fine after my father brought my crazy ass sister to dinner, and then she got beat up by my baby daddy's mom for talking crazy. This was honestly all too much, and I just wanted to get away from all of them. Shai came around and reached for my hand. Instead of accepting his help, I used the table and moved around him.

In my opinion, everyone had allowed this shit to go way farther than it needed to, especially Shai. Besides my daddy, he was the whole reason she was even over there showing her ass. Instead of handling that shit, he let it escalate to the point that his mama beat her bloody.

"Mama, I'll call you in a little bit," I said, noticing the way she was watching the interaction.

Despite how fast I was moving, Shai still managed to beat me to the door and grabbed my coat before I could. He tried to slip it on my shoulders, but I jerked away.

"Zuri—"

"No! I don't even want to talk about it. Just get me home, please." It had already been a whole circus, and I wasn't trying to add to the mess. I didn't even know if I wanted to speak to Shai at all. Surprisingly, he just nodded stiffly and opened the door for me.

The ride home was much different than the one over. It was completely silent, with no music and no talking. I spent the whole time staring out the window with my back to him. I honestly didn't know how such a nice night could've turned into this, but at the same time, I knew exactly how. It was like the universe was trying to tell me something because every time I thought me and Shai had moved past our issues, they returned, making me feel dumb for even thinking we could work.

When he finally pulled up to my house, I didn't even wait for him to open the door for me. I hurried to take off my seat belt and scurried up to my door with my keys already in hand. Shai was right on my heels, though, and forced his way in before I could shut the door behind me.

"I said I don't wanna talk about it. Just...give me some time."

"If you think I'm leavin' this muhfucka tonight, you out yo' goddamn mind," he said and calmly locked the door.

Letting out a low groan, I kicked out of my heels and started toward my bedroom. The last thing I wanted was to wake up Sevyn, and since he didn't want to leave, the least I could do was try to make sure we didn't get too loud.

Once I got to my room, I started removing my jewelry. Next came the pins out of my hair while Shai watched from the door. "Say what you wanna say," I told him without turning around.

"I don't got shit to say. I'm tryna figure out what your issue is, love."

My eyebrows damn near touched as I whipped around. I grew even more confused, seeing that he had stripped out of his jacket and had untucked his shirt. I didn't even know what to address first, but I decided on the obvious.

"What are you doin'?" By then, he was removing his cufflinks. He slipped them into his pocket and started unbuttoning his shirt.

"I told you I'm not leaving. We've been doing enough of that running shit. Let's get to the bottom of whatever it is that's bothering you."

I chuckled and shook my head at that. "What's bothering me? Besides the fact that you were in a relationship with my sister and could've been her child's father, nothing really," I said in exaggerated nonchalance.

We all were well aware of the elephant in the room, and it was crazy that he was acting like it didn't exist and I was tripping for nothing.

"So, this is about Kendra still?" He tilted his head and came out of his shirt.

I had to take a few calming breaths because his tone and demeanor were both pissing me off, and I didn't want to seem like the erratic one when he was clearly out of his mind.

"No! This is about how every time things seem to be going good with us, she pops up, reminding me that y'all were together and in the most insane ways. I don't want to spend the rest of my life feeling guilty because she still thinks she has claims to you."

"You don't think that's what she wants?" he asked, slowly coming toward me like he was afraid to make any sudden movements. When I didn't immediately dodge his embrace, he circled his arms around me. "Look, I know you're stressed out, and this shit with Kendra ain't helping, but I'm not about to let her ruin this. You and I both know besides this shit with her, we're fucking perfect together. We made something perfect together, and he deserves us both there. We can't let her fuck up what we have."

The wall I'd started building on the way home was already coming down. The truth was, I wanted to be with Shai. I really wanted us to work, but Kendra and my father weren't obstacles that *could easily be avoided. My head dropped, and Shai lifted it with a finger tucked under my chin.*

"Look, just let me handle Kendra, okay? I'll make sure she doesn't bother us again," he promised, pressing his lips against mine.

I didn't know how he planned to stop her, but the distraction of his kiss and his hands roaming my body clouded my judgment, and I didn't even care to ask.

SEVYN

"*I wish I was there to see that shit! Shai's mama is my type of bitch for real!*"

I laughed until I noticed the look on Zuri's face. She clearly didn't find any of this shit funny despite how hilarious it was to me. From what she'd told me, Kendra had that ass whooping coming, and thankfully, Shai's mama was willing to do it since Zuri couldn't. Obviously, the girl had gone without proper discipline from her own mama, so Queen just gave her what she needed.

"*You think that shit funny, Sevyn?*"

"*You don't? She was over at that lady's house after she wronged her son, talking reckless. And low key, yo' daddy ain't shit for bringing her. I mean, what the fuck was he thinking?*" *I frowned, thinking about how Mr. Kadeem could do some shit like that.*

It was like he was choosing one daughter over the other, but in my opinion, he had been giving everybody but Zuri the benefit of the doubt since she was a teenager. That was one of the reasons I respected Ms. Zora so much. It took a strong ass woman to deal with a man like him, especially when he wasn't even helping financially with their child.

"*I don't even know. He's been acting funny since I told him I* was divorcing Deshawn." She fluttered her fingers dismissively and took a sip of her pink lemonade.

I couldn't even do shit but shake my head. I didn't understand how he was on a nigga's side who had clearly been mistreating his daughter but wanted to give Shai a hard time for some shit she had no control over.

"I know you wanna bring everybody together to do the whole family thing, but you might need to cut his ass off for real this time and just let him have his ratchet ass love child. 'Cause, at this point, he's giving toxic ex."

I felt bad for my girl. She was literally so close to having everything she wanted and deserved, but shit kept getting in the way. First, it was Deshawn's stupid ass, and now it was her own father and sister. To some extent, I could understand why Kendra felt some type of way, but she really didn't have anybody to blame but herself for cheating on Shai in the first place. She was clearly one of those dumb ass women who didn't know what they had until it was gone. It was too late, though, because Zuri had her baby daddy wrapped around her finger, and no matter how hard she tried, Shai wasn't letting up off my bestie.

"Yeah, my mama mad as fuck at him too. She done cussed his ass out like three times since last night."

"Girl, you know Ms. Zora don't play!" I cracked up.

I could already imagine her getting in his ass. Even Zuri had to join me because she knew her mama better than anyone.

"Yeah, well, he's been calling all morning, trying to get me to meet up with him. I'll probably just block his ass until after I have the baby because I'm not tryna get this far just for my family to be the reason behind me losing my baby." Shrugging, she took a bite of her chicken salad while I pushed my plate away. The pasta I'd ordered had me stuffed, but I still wanted to order some dessert for later, and I already knew what I was going to get.

"Shit, maybe while your baby daddy handling yo' crazy ass sister, he can get yo' daddy to stop texting you too," I suggested nonchalantly, even though I hoped he did. Catching the eye of our *waitress, I waved her over while Zuri seemed to mull the thought over in her head.*

"I wish, but hell, he's barely handling her, so no need to add my daddy to the mix." She continued eating just as the waitress made it to our table.

"Umm, can you get me a couple slices of strawberry cheesecake to go?"

"Oooh, that sounds good! I'll take one of those too." Zuri's greedy ass lit up. "Matter fact, make it two," she added, holding up her fingers for emphasis.

"That's right. You better feed my nephew," I teased as my phone vibrated.

The smile instantly slipped from my face when I saw a picture text of Zuri and me from Detective Hill. "Uhhh, I'ma have to eat and run, girl. This damn lawyer wants to meet." I pulled a few bills out and dropped them on the table to cover both our food before climbing to my feet.

"Hold on. What about your cheesecake?"

"Just take it home for me. This won't take long." I was really glad I'd driven myself there because I didn't want Zuri coming along with me.

Shit, I didn't want anybody to know what I had going on, not when it was so unlike me. Zuri looked thoroughly confused as I ran off, and I hoped to keep it that way for everybody's sake.

I pulled up to the isolated location that Detective Hill had sent to me with an attitude. As soon as I stepped out of my car, he came from around a set of bushes, and my nose turned up at the sight of him.

"Ms. Ellis, you're a hard woman to get in touch with. Didn't I tell you that you needed to check in with me? This shit won't just go away because you're avoiding me."

"I'm not avoiding you. I just haven't had a chance to do what you asked." I clenched my teeth to stop myself from saying what I really wanted to say.

Ever since I'd taken my dumb ass up to the police station with

Brian, he'd been hounding me to set up Rome so that we could get Tramel's plug. Somehow, Brian had tricked me into becoming an informant just so that Tyrese, my stylists, and I could walk away from this shit unscathed. I honestly felt like they couldn't put the drugs and money they found on all of us, but with the way the police department was set up, we could all go down. As real of a bitch as I was, I wasn't trying to be in anybody's orange jumpsuit. Besides, it wasn't like Tramel was innocent, and since I didn't have any proof that he was the one who tried to kill me, he'd virtually have gotten away with ruining my life if I didn't do this.

Detective Hill smirked and moved closer. "And why haven't you been able to do that?"

"It's not as easy as calling him up for a meeting when I'm sure he knows exactly what the fuck Tramel did! They're not stupid. They won't fuck with me with this damn case hanging over my head!" I didn't get how he couldn't understand the stupidity of their little sting operation. There wasn't a chance in hell that Rome would come anywhere near me, let alone discuss some illegal shit after I'd just had work found in my shop.

"See, I don't think you're even trying, Sevyn, and I hate that for you... well, you and your co-workers. Do you think I'm playing? I'll continue with these charges, and while y'all in jail doin' hair for commissary, I'll get somebody else to get this done! Although, I don't know how easy it'll be for ole Tyrese to make it by doing hair in a male prison. Niggas ain't as friendly to feminine muhfuckas in there as you would think. He'll fuck around and get passed around until his ass is as wide as the Grand Canyon. Is that what you want?" he asked, smirking at the horror on my face.

"No! I'll do it just... give me some time, okay? I'll at least need access to my home and shop so I look legit."

He tilted his head and studied me without speaking for a few uncomfortable seconds before nodding.

"Okay. I'll see what I can do, and in the meantime, answer whenever I call you. I don't want to have to pull up on you again."

He backed away and disappeared through the same bushes he'd come from, leaving me with an eerie ass feeling.

I already didn't know how he'd found Zuri and me, but I wasn't trying to have him make his presence known the next time. I stood there for a few minutes longer, sucking in big gulps of frigid air as I tried to calm my racing heart. Fucking around with Tramel, I'd gotten myself in some shit that I wasn't just going to easily walk away from. Shit!

Whatever magic Detective Hill worked had me back in my shop within days. Since no one had been there after the raid, it was still fucked up, and there was shit tossed everywhere. I clutched my phone as I walked through, taking in the damage, when the bell over the door had me damn near jumping out of my skin.

"Ahhhh!"

"Ahhh—bitch!" Tyrese's hand flew to his chest, and he glared at me through thick lashes. "Fuck you screaming for when you called me, hoe?" he said, tossing his thirty-inch bust down over his shoulder.

"My bad, I-I'm still a little shook, I guess," I mumbled, looking at the floor.

"Well, that's understandable. I mean, you did get shot here." He took off his crossbody and walked toward me with open arms. "You poor thing. With all this other shit going on, I forgot all about the fact that coming here could give you PTSD or something."

I fell into his chest, not even realizing that the familiar scent of his Valentino cologne would be so comforting. The detectives had kept us from interacting, but once I turned informant, they lifted our no contact. It was right on time, too, because things in my life were spiraling out of control. I hadn't even considered that coming back to the place where I was shot could affect me, but I was jumpy as fuck.

"God, I missed you." My voice cracked as I squeezed him tighter.

"I missed you too, girl! You know you're the only one who gets me. All these other bitches just be jealous," he teased, making me laugh at his conceited ass. "Are you okay, though? I know this shit

gotta be weighing on you. You're not even a snitching type of bitch, and they want you to snitch on a nigga that done already tried to kill you? That's craaaaazy work."

"Hell no, I'm not okay. This shit got me all the way fucked up." I sighed, dropping into one of the chairs.

"I'm surprised a nigga like Zaaaaaakir is even letting you do something like this. What his fine ass been talkin' 'bout?"

I sucked my teeth and avoided eye contact. With everything going on, I hadn't told Tyrese about me and Zaakir falling out.

"Uh uh, bitch, spill," he pressed, twisting his lips.

I went ahead and gave him a quick rundown of what happened the morning I stopped fucking with Zaakir. By the time I was finished, his dramatic ass had fallen onto the chair next to me, clutching his imaginary pearls.

"I don't know who I'm more mad at, you for being so secretive and losing our man, or his ass for taking it that far." He clicked his tongue, annoyed. *"Do you think he fucked somebody else?"* He suddenly gasped.

I'd only been half listening, but the second he mentioned cheating, my ears perked up. Cheating hadn't really been my biggest concern when he brought his dumb ass in. In fact, I was just so worried about him shitting on my feelings that I hadn't considered it at all, but now that Tyrese had said something, I couldn't help but wonder. As many times as Tramel had gone out and cheated, only to come back with an attitude at me, I should've seen the signs right in my face. I shook off the hurt that had suddenly crept up on me and rolled my eyes.

"It don't even matter. I'm not fuckin' with him or no nigga for that matter. I'm literally on a nigga detox until further notice." I sighed, making his face turn up in disbelief. *"I'm serious. If I get us outta this mess, I don't think I'll ever talk to another nigga. Shit, I'm probably bouta turn gay 'cause these niggas ain't shit."*

"Ain't that the truth?" he agreed.

"You should try it too. We can be each others' support person."

"Uh, no. I'm good, love. Enjoy. Fuck I look like turning down a

*man that wanna fuck me and spend money? Tuh! You on yo' own
with that."* He cackled, and I waved his crazy ass off.

*He could continue to fuck around and find out, but I was done
with that, especially since Zaakir hadn't even tried to apologize at
all. As mad as I was at first, I held a small amount of hope that he
would come to his senses, but when he didn't, I had to force myself to
let that shit go. Besides, if he ever found out what I had going on, he
definitely wouldn't be trying to fuck with me... he'd kill my ass.*

ZAAKIR

The results of my tests had come back, and thankfully, my shit was clean, or else I'd have to kill Britney's stupid ass. I just knew that next time, I would be more careful when it came to who I stuck my dick in. Knowing I was clean, though, had me a lot less stressed, so I could focus on getting money. Shai had insisted on bringing me into this deal his pops made. It was going to be an easy two hundred and fifty grand. While it probably wouldn't have sounded like much to Casa, I didn't turn down shit with more than three zeroes. He was already feeling some type of way about us working with Giorgio anyway, so he was going to talk shit regardless of if it was a quarter mil or not.

I pulled up to the spot and scanned the area for Shai before checking the time. We still had a few minutes before we were supposed to be there, so I wasn't tripping, but it wasn't like his ass not to be early as fuck. I waited another minute or so and dialed his number when I still didn't see any headlights pulling up.

"Where the fuck you at?"

"I'm pulling up now," he said and hung up.

A second later, I saw his headlights coming my way. When he came to a stop, I checked my gun before getting out and meeting him at my trunk just as another car crept in front of us. Two middle-aged men climbed out and stopped in front of their car. The building we were meeting behind had just enough light for us to see that they were black, and I chortled to myself. It figured Giorgio's racist ass would have us doing this shit to another nigga, but I wasn't about to try to gain morals when we were already there.

"Where the money at?" I didn't hesitate to ask. This shouldn't have been something that took a very long time.

"Pictures first!" the driver shouted back, and I instantly shared a look with Shai.

We didn't know what exactly we were extorting these niggas for. We only knew that it was extremely incriminating, and if I was getting a quarter mil for it, I didn't give a fuck.

Shai went into his pocket and tossed over a manila envelope, which the other dude caught in midair. The way he'd casually handed that shit over let me know he had backups, and they must've known, too, because they tossed two duffel bags at our feet. While dude went through the pictures, I knelt to check out the cash. I flipped through each bundle with a UV flashlight and did the same with the next bag.

"You ain't gotta do all that. The bills legit." The one with the pictures huffed impatiently, but I didn't even acknowledge that goofy shit. He was a fool if he thought I was going to take a chance with some niggas I ain't know. It took a little time, but once I'd checked every bill, I zipped it back up and gave Shai a nod. "Okay, cool. You satisfied? Now, where the copies at?"

"You crazy as hell if you thought I'd bring every copy I got." Shai grit, pulling his phone out and tapping the screen a few times. "The others will be at your office in about one minute." On cue, their phones began to trill less than a minute later, and they got the confirmation that the pictures were there.

"Okay, and how do we know that's it and y'all won't try this shit again?"

Shai shrugged. "You just gon' have to take my word for it, I guess."

"The fuck!"

"Look, I'm telling yo' ass I gave you everything, but if you wanna keep talking, you gon' be doing it with that nigga, not me." Shai pointed at the man's partner and reached to pick up one of the bags while I grabbed the other one. *"Now, get the fuck outta here,"* he ordered, standing upright.

They stared each other down until, eventually, they retreated to the car and drove off. We stayed put until their lights disappeared around the corner, and I couldn't help but grin cockily. We'd virtually just made a quarter of a million dollars in under five minutes! I wasn't fucking with Giorgio like that, but I couldn't deny that he'd come through on this deal. Shai sent another text before popping the trunk, and we threw our bags inside. We dapped each other up and went to our separate vehicles. The plan was to meet back up at Shai's crib in an hour. To buy some time, I stopped through the drive-thru of Chick-fil-A.

Exactly an hour later, I pulled up to Shai's crib, and instantly, my face balled up as I was blinded by the lights from multiple police vehicles. Without thinking, I jumped out and hurried over just as they dragged a cuffed Shai into the backseat of one of their squad cars.

"Aye, what the fuck y'all arresting him for!" I snapped, pushing my way through the group of officers littering his driveway.

"Zaakir A'santi?" one asked, butchering my name as he stopped me.

"Zaakir A'santi, muhfucka!" I quickly corrected, looking over his shoulder to see the others going into his trunk. My soul was instantly crushed when they pulled out the duffle bags.

Sighing, my head dropped because there was no way this was just a regular traffic stop. Somebody had told them about the deal, and the only nigga who should've known about it was Giorgio. My arm being bent behind my back snapped me back into the moment, and I fought against the tight grip he had on me.

"Well, Zaakir A'santi, you and your cousin over there are under arrest for extortion! Congratufuckinglations!"

To be continued...

SHAI

I glanced at my watch, noting that I'd been sitting in this fucking interrogation room for damn near two hours. Despite the rage brewing inside me, I kept my face neutral while one of the detectives questioning me looked like he was about to explode. He'd been the more aggressive of the two, shouting and slamming angry fists on the table every time I didn't give him the answers he wanted while his partner tried to butter me up. I wasn't falling for either of their acts, though. Casa had us trained not to speak when being questioned unless we were asking for a lawyer. Plus, I wanted to know exactly what they thought they knew.

When they mentioned the extortion and found the money, I'd immediately been under the impression that Giorgio had set us up. That was until they began to drop pictures of damn near every meeting and even some of him with the other bosses. It was clear they'd been following us, or at the very least following that nigga, for some time. As pissed off as I was that we'd been roped into his shit, I was willing to eat whatever they hit me with if they released Zaakir. This whole thing was my deal, and it was only right that I took the heat for it.

"Are you fuckin' listening? You're caught red-handed, and in addition to your ties to this crime family, you're looking at twenty-plus years!" he barked, leaning across the table. "You think your little baby mama will wait that long for you? I doubt it. She'll be on to the next man with fat pockets! Shit, she'll probably be getting passed around the very same crime family that your mom used to—"

I'd been tolerating his mouth for way too long, but the mention of Zuri and my mama was the last straw. Before he could fully get the words out, I slammed his head down on the metal table, not giving a damn about the consequences of assaulting a police officer. Fuck it, they were already trying to charge me with some bullshit, so I may as well get some frustration out and let him know that level of disrespect wouldn't be tolerated.

They were both so shocked by the sudden attack that they froze, unsure of how to handle the situation, before his partner finally jumped out of his seat.

"You motherfucker! I'm gonna bury your ass in prison!" the big mouth shouted once he got his bearings.

He pretended like his partner holding him back was the only reason he couldn't reach me, but I could see the fear in his eyes. He definitely hadn't expected me to lay a finger on him, and that was their problem right there. They felt like their badges were pieces of armor that allowed them a certain amount of protection, but he'd obviously never met a nigga like me.

Smirking at the threat, I relaxed back into my seat. Embarrassment had to be eating his ass up while I was more amused than I'd been the entire time I'd been there. I watched while he put up an overexaggerated fight, waiting for the moment when his partner finally got him out of the room so I could ask for my lawyer.

The door swinging open had all our eyes shooting that way, and I immediately frowned at the sight of Giorgio's ass walking in. His presence put a stop to the struggle between the two, making me chuckle bitterly as he nodded for them both to leave.

"I want extra for this shit, G!" Dude stopped at the threshold and pointed at his temple, where a lump was already beginning to form. I didn't know what he expected, but he was met with a steely glare that had his partner pushing him out the door.

"What type of fuckin' games you playin', Giorgio?" I grit once they were gone, and he dropped into the chair across from me. His calm demeanor made it even more apparent that this whole shit was his doing, and even though I was relieved, I couldn't help wanting to knock his fucking head off his shoulders.

"No games. I just needed to make sure you and Zaakir were prepared for any situation." He folded his hands on top of the table with a shrug. "*This* entire department down to the fuckers who work the desk are in my pocket, but I can't say the same for the others, and I need you and your cousin to be able to handle the type of shit they'll throw at you to try to get you to talk. You both did well besides Zaakir's shit talking and you physically attacking Detective Baker. Lucky for you, he's led by greed, but you need to do better about controlling your temper. These fuckers will say anything to get a reaction out of you. Next time, mine and your lawyer's name are all you have to say," he advised while I tried hard not to put my hands on him. This whole setup had been a complete waste of time, and I fully intended to keep my cut and give Zaakir his.

"This the last time you gon' pull some bullshit like this, or I'm done fuckin' with you," I told him, standing to my feet. "I don't give a fuck if this shit is fake either. I want my damn money back too." Without waiting for him to speak, I headed out of the room, mugging every police officer I saw on my way down the hall.

As if on cue, Zaakir emerged from one of the other interrogation rooms, and just like me, his face was twisted into an evil scowl. He waited until I reached him and fell into step beside me, talking shit the whole time. I was too irritated to even tell his ass to chill. All I wanted to do was get the fuck out of there. Thankfully, we made it outside without him getting into a scuffle with any of the officers, and Giorgio met us out on the stairs where my OG was just arriving.

"You got us fucked up, Gio!" she hopped out, already going off.

Just like always, she and Casa were two steps ahead of everything because I knew they hadn't allowed Zaakir to make a call either. She was dressed for a fight and quickly raced up the stairs with Casa right on her heels.

"Queen—" He tried to explain, and she cut his ass right off with a strong hook to the jaw. His bodyguards appeared out of nowhere and immediately went to stop her next attack, but Casa already had his gun out.

"I wish the fuck y'all would lay a finger on my sister!"

"Sammie, Dean, it's okay." Giorgio massaged his jaw as he pushed them aside.

"Yeah, you better get these muhfuckas!" Queen asserted, sizing them up like they were toddlers instead of grown ass men who could bench press her with one hand. "You're lucky I don't kill y'all asses myself for this shit! Why the fuck is my son and nephew coming out of a police station? When you left, you said you were going to handle some business but conveniently left out that my son being hemmed up was what the fuck that business was!"

"Amore, there was nothing to tell. This was just a little... drill, if you will, to ensure they know what to do in such cases."

My face was already balled up for a few reasons. One was that they were talking about me like I was a little nigga, and the other was because I caught on to my mama saying he'd left like he'd been at her crib before coming there. But it balled up even more at the term of endearment that seemed to be lost on everyone else but me.

"Fuck you talkin' 'bout? These niggas as solid as they come! I know 'cause I trained them!" Casa fumed, pounding his chest with his free hand since he was still holding tightly to his gun. "You wasted time and my fuckin' tax dollars on this bullshit!"

"What you consider a waste of time and resources, I consider reassurance. Don't forget that Shai is heading up the largest organization in Chicago now because of my blood, but that doesn't mean he doesn't have to prove himself at times. It just is what it is, but both of them are fine. If anything, they caused more damage to those fuckers." He nodded toward the precinct with a chuckle, but my mama only snorted in reply.

"Look, can we just get the fuck from around here? We can talk about this shit at the crib or something 'cause this mutha-fucka got me itching."

Zaakir followed the statement up with a scratching motion, and my mama's eyes shot his way. "I get that you been through some shit tonight, so I'm gon' let that one slide." She then turned her attention back to Giorgio. "And you! Giorgio De'Luca, I don't give a damn what you deem a reassurance! Don't you ever do no shit like this again, or I'll—"

"Queen, my love, you're upset, but that will be the last time you threaten or put your hands on me. Shai and Zaakir are fine, but if he's going to take over with his cousin at his side, then he will undergo the same training that I had to and every other De'Luca man did." He spoke sternly, and I was surprised by the way my OG ultimately backed down. That, along with the obvious, was just another indication that shit between them had gone beyond coming together for the sole purpose of me taking over.

"Go ahead, nephew. I got her." Casa nodded me off and mumbled something I couldn't hear to Zaakir's ass.

Both annoyed and disgusted, I started down the stairs, ready to get the fuck away from the police and their asses. I hadn't even noticed that both mine and Zaakir's cars were parked at the curb running. I guess that's where his men had been coming from, but I wasn't even trying to think that hard about how Giorgio and his people had pulled this shit off. Instead, I climbed behind the wheel of my car and was only slightly pleased with the sight of one bag of our money resting on my passenger seat. Pulling off, I let my family disappear in my rearview and headed home, setting my phone on DND. I needed a minute away from all their asses.

ZURI

I woke up to featherlight kisses on my face and neck, and when I opened my eyes, I was surprised to see the sun was just barely up, letting me know how early it was. Of course, my horny ass didn't give a damn about the hour when my baby daddy woke me up with his lips on me. I immediately wrapped my arms around his neck and pulled him closer with a low sigh.

"Get yo' freaky ass up. Ain't nobody tryna hump on you, girl." His voice filled with amusement that had my eyes snapping open and my bottom lip poked out.

"Why'd you wake me up then?" I whined, more annoyed than anything that he hadn't woken me up for some mind-blowing sex. That only made his grin widen at my petulance.

"Quit being so grumpy. You already know if I put this dick on you, yo' ass gon' go right back to sleep, and I need you to get up and get some clothes on. I got a surprise for you." I was about to object until he got to the part about my surprise, and my eyes narrowed suspiciously.

"What is it?"

He snorted, but the smirk never left his face. "That defeats the whole purpose of a surprise, love. You gon' have to get yo' ass up to find out, and you ain't got a lot of time, so get movin'." He checked his Rolex and then pecked my lips before standing to his full height and reaching out to help me up.

Tossing the covers off me, I accepted his hand and allowed him to pull me into a sitting position and then onto my feet as excitement bubbled through me. I didn't know what to expect, but knowing Shai, it was definitely going to be a good surprise, and I couldn't wait to see it.

"Should I put on something casual or dressy?" I yawned, glad that we were at my house so I had more options to pick from.

"Dress comfortable. Some leggings or sweats should be cool. I don't want my baby feeling restricted." His head was down as his fingers moved swiftly across his phone screen, so he didn't notice the way my face fell.

I couldn't imagine what type of surprise required me to wear some damn leggings or sweatpants unless there was food involved. The thought perked me right back up, and I wasted no time pulling out a Nike hoodie with matching joggers.

After handling my hygiene, I quickly applied body butter, taking extra care to moisturize my belly before getting dressed and sliding into a pair of black Vapor Max. The whole time, a fully dressed Shai sat on the edge of my bed with his face still buried in his phone.

"Ready," I chimed, gaining his attention.

He looked me up and down in a way that made me feel like I was naked instead of fully clothed, and I couldn't help blushing. One thing Shai was going to do was make me feel desirable with little to no effort, and I loved that for me. He licked his lips sexily and stood, tucking his phone into his pocket as he closed the distance between us.

"Damn, you look good as fuck," he complimented, pulling me to him. My body immediately melted against his. "You smell good enough to eat, too." He'd buried his face in my neck, so his voice came out muffled. "Fuck around and take yo' fine ass right back to bed."

Had he not already gotten me so excited about my surprise, I would've instantly stripped and let him do just that. Instead, I snapped right out of the trance he'd put me in and quickly wiggled away.

"Aht aht! It's too late for all that. I'm invested now. I want my surprise." That had him chuckling, and despite my own smirk, I was serious as hell.

"Okay, okay, you got that, but you gon' have to put this on before we go." He held up one of my silk scarves with a mischievous grin.

Squealing, I couldn't help but wonder what he had planned as I clapped and spun around so he could put the blindfold on. Instead of guiding me through the house by hand, he carried me down to what I knew was his car from the lingering scent of his cologne. I spent the entire drive trying to pry clues about where we were going out of him, but he wasn't budging. His slick ass distracted me by bringing up the fact that we had yet to give the baby a name. We really hadn't discussed anything, but considering it was a boy, I was already planning to make him a junior, which is what I told him.

"Really?" He sounded genuinely shocked, but I could hear the smile in his voice.

"Yes, really. I love your name. It'll be cute for y'all to share it," I gushed. "Plus, we can always get creative with the next one."

I'd only been half joking, but he didn't hesitate to agree, tenderly kissing the back of my hand. "Yeah, 'cause I'm definitely tryna follow up with a little princess as soon as possible."

"Tuh, there's no way I'm letting you sit me right back down after I have your big-headed son. My coochie gon' need at least a two-year break before I pop out another baby," I denied, even though I was already imagining what our baby girl would look like. The truth was, I couldn't wait to have all his big-headed babies.

"We'll see," he said, sounding far from convinced as the car crawled to a stop.

I listened silently as he shut the engine off and climbed out.

Excitement shot through me, and I had to resist the urge to snatch my blindfold off, knowing we had arrived.

Shai reached my side quickly and pulled the door open, reaching in to help me out. "You ready?" he asked after shuffling me a few feet away and hugging me from behind.

"Yessss..." I cheesed, tilting my head in anticipation, but my voice quickly trailed off as he removed the scarf, and a big ass airplane came into view. The smiling attendants stood on either side of the stairs along with the pilot. Gasping, I looked at Shai, who was wearing an accomplished grin of his own. "What?"

He shrugged and grasped my hand into his. "I feel like we deserve a getaway, just you, me, and my lil' man. Consider it a baby moon or whatever they call that shit."

"But—"

"You trust me, right?" Shai cut me off.

"Yes, but—"

"Then you know your man already took care of everything." As he spoke, he ushered me closer to the plane. "All you need to worry about is relaxing."

On cue, each of the attendants came and began to unload the car, which surprised the hell out of me. Obviously, Shai had really taken care of everything because they had my pink suitcase along with my purse.

"You managed to do all this while I was asleep?" I asked, getting teary eyed.

I didn't know what my surprise was going to be, but the last thing I expected was a trip on a private jet. My emotions were getting the best of me, as usual.

"Small shit to a giant." He winked, flashing a charming grin that had my panties soaked. I knew without a doubt that I was going to suck the skin off his dick as soon as I got him alone.

SHAI

I ignored another call from my OG and continued to brush my teeth. She, along with her baby daddy, had been blowing my phone up for the last two days, but they were both on my shitlist until further notice. Although she didn't have anything to do with the shit he pulled, her sneaky ass relationship with that nigga had me looking at her sideways. I for damn sure wanted an explanation as to why she was creeping around with him again after all the shit she claimed he'd done, but that would have to wait until I made it home. I wasn't about to let my parent's bullshit fuck up my vacation.

Despite their constant calls, our time in Jamaica had been relaxing and was just the time away that we needed. It seemed like every time Zuri and I took two steps forward, some outside source set our shit five steps back. Being in our own little bubble and away from the drama back home had us locked back in, though. The peace had Zuri more carefree than she'd been since our time in Miami, and the sun, in addition to the multiple orgasms I'd been blessing her with, had her glowing and relaxed.

From where I stood, I could see her completely naked and wrapped up in the white sheets. I couldn't help but smile, knowing my plan had worked. I quickly finished brushing my teeth and climbed into bed, not wanting to interrupt her sleep, but we were already running late. I kissed her full, pouty lips, causing her to stir slightly before snuggling against my body.

"You gotta get up, love. We're already running behind," I finally said after another kiss did nothing to rouse her.

Releasing a moan, she burrowed deeper into the bed, this time wrapping her smooth leg around me to pull me closer, and I chuckled lowly.

She already had me second-guessing whether I really wanted to leave the bed, let alone the room, with that little move right there. If I hadn't put so much thought and effort into the day, I would've been trying to fall asleep between her thighs again.

"Ten more minutes," she whined as I gently bit her neck.

"You always tryna con yo' way into some extra sleep when I got plans." My lips spread into a smirk, still pressed lightly against her skin.

"And you're always planning activities after putting that devil dick on me," she shot back irritably.

I couldn't help laughing at the truth. I'd definitely been fucking her every chance I got, but it was hard to keep my hands to myself. Her pussy was addictive as fuck, and no matter how disciplined I tried to be, it was no use.

"You got me, love, but this'll be the last time." The lie rolled effortlessly off my tongue.

She let out a grunt, knowing damn well I wasn't telling the truth. Still, she wrestled herself out of the sheets, and my eyes landed on her full breasts. For a second, I considered taking her chocolate nipples into my mouth but thought better of it, seeing the look she was throwing my way.

"Don't even think about it," she grumbled, rolling her eyes before scooting to the edge of the bed.

It was clearly a struggle, and while she normally would've asked for assistance, her attitude had her stubborn ass struggling to do it herself. She finally made it to her feet and wobbled into the bathroom, slamming the door behind her, but I didn't even trip because I knew once she saw her surprise, she'd be in a much better mood.

An hour later, she still had a slight attitude as we walked hand in hand along the beach. She looked amazing in a bright orange dress with her hair pulled back and covered with a straw hat. Since it was so hot, she'd opted not to wear any makeup, and her natural glow made it hard to keep my eyes and hands off her.

"Awwww, baby!" she squealed, snatching my attention away from her ass that was giving extra jiggle beneath her dress.

We'd finally made it to the dock where a yacht was waiting with a sign on the side that read, *Welcome aboard, Zuri.* Her eyes watered as she threw her arms around me, hugging me tightly before taking a step back to take another look at the boat.

"I can't believe this. A private jet and a yacht, all in the same week! You're really outdoing yourself, Mr. A'santi."

"Oh yeah? So does that mean yo' onery ass ain't mad no more?" I chided, giving her body a little squeeze. Pulling away, she playfully slapped my arm and sucked her teeth.

"I was not mad." Her phony ass didn't hesitate to lie, and before I could call her out, she had my hand, pulling me toward the yacht. "Now, come on so I can see it before they fuck around and leave us."

Now, she was the one rushing, but I let her make it since I knew she was so excited.

"Welcome to the Delilah!" The captain and two staff members greeted us with a couple of fruity ass drinks before guiding us aboard.

Zuri oohed and ahhed as they gave us a tour, completely smitten with every inch of the luxurious yacht, just like I knew she would. Everything from the Brazilian cherry wood that covered the floors to the cushy lower bunk with a jacuzzi screamed opulence, and for the thousands I'd spent, it was well worth it to see her excitement. We finished the tour in the lounge area near the swim deck while they brought our overnight bags on.

"This is amazing!" Zuri gushed, tossing her head back with a satisfied moan that had my dick stirring. "You're really tryna have me slurred out and bustin' it open for you this whole trip, huh?" she joked, but her eyes were full of lust as they landed on me.

Shrugging, I set my glass down before pulling her feet into my lap and pressing my thumbs into her arches. Another moan had me ready to tear her clothes off right there, but I resisted the urge, knowing they'd be calling us for lunch soon.

"We aim to please, baby." I smirked. "But, for real, I'm happy you're enjoying yourself. You deserve it... shit, we both do." My voice dropped just thinking about everything we would be returning to once our vacation was over. I quickly shook that shit off, though, not wanting it to ruin our peaceful moment.

"Yeah, because soon we won't have a minute to ourselves, let alone time to take a vacation." She sighed, rubbing her belly with her free hand as a smile tugged at her lips.

I couldn't lie; the arrival of our son had me both excited and terrified at the same time. I'd been prepping myself for his presence since finding out he was mine, but I still didn't feel like I was ready. Would my fatherly instincts kick in immediately? My ass hadn't ever really even been around kids, let alone been responsible for one, but I knew I wanted everything that came with my son—the good, the bad, and the ugly.

Giorgio had given me the tools I needed to know what *not* to do, and while Casa was a father figure, I wouldn't call him the best model to adhere to. In addition to my own feelings of inadequacy, there was still the matter of Zuri and me. Without a doubt, I wanted our child to have what neither of us did growing up, and that was both of us in a home together. She still hadn't agreed to us being under the same roof, but I also hadn't been applying the amount of pressure I should've since I'd been so busy.

"Aww, is that your nervous face? I don't think I've ever seen you anything less than confident and suave," Zuri teased, snapping me out of my thoughts with an amused expression on her beautiful face.

"Not at all, love." I quickly shook my head in denial. "I'm just thinking…" Her eyebrows shot up curiously at my vague response.

"About?"

Sighing, I moved my hands up her calf, stopping at her thigh and giving it a squeeze as our eyes locked. "What type of house I'ma get us." I immediately felt her stiffen uncomfortably, just like every other time I broached the subject. She attempted to remove her feet from my lap, but I held her in place. She'd been running from this conversation long enough, though, and I wasn't taking no for an answer. "You don't think lil' Shai deserves for us to be in the same house? What sense does it make to have us bouncing between houses when we already damn near live together as is?"

The question was rhetorical, but she still took it upon herself to answer. "It makes perfect sense, considering that I *just* got out of a situation with a man who—"

"Ain't me." I cut her off, unable to keep my expression neutral. "Stop comparing me to that nigga 'cause we're not the same. I been in your corner since the day I met you. Ain't no switching up for me, baby. We locked the fuck in, and I ain't lettin' up off you whether we live under the same roof or not. The plan is marriage and raising our baby together in the home we're gonna grow old in. Don't let that nigga's fuck ups stop you from allowing me to give you the life you deserve."

Her fear of having a repeat of the shit that went down with her bitch ass husband had me ready to go beat his ass again. Panic crossed her face, and I could damn near see her heart pounding out of her chest, so I toned it down a little, cupping her chin and bringing my face close to hers.

"Zuri, I love you. I love him," I emphasized, looking down at her stomach. "I just want a fair chance to show you how much. I can't say every day gon' be perfect 'cause that shit would be a lie. Some days, I'm gon' get on yo' nerves, and some days, you gon' irritate the fuck out of me, but I ain't ever gon' do shit to hurt you." A tear slipped out, and I quickly wiped it away.

"So, you won't even leave on the days I'm irritating the fuck out of you?" she finally spoke with a hint of a smile on her lips.

"Shiiiit, I'll make sure our crib is so big that me and SJ can go kick it in a completely separate side until we ready to be bothered with you again." I shrugged, making her giggle, even though I was only half kidding. I already knew for a fact that whatever house we chose was going to be big enough for the six kids I planned to trap her ass with.

Shaking her head, she sighed and narrowed her eyes as she threatened. "I swear you better not make me regret this, Shai A'santi."

"Never," I vowed, crashing my lips against hers. I was going to make sure I got her the house of her dreams, and when the time was right, I was going to bless her with my last name, too.

SEVYN

I smiled as the sounds in my shop filled my ears. It had only been a few weeks, but I'd missed the gossip, music, and overall vibe that being within those four walls gave me. We'd only been back open for a couple of days since it took forever to get the place cleaned up after the raid, but we were already back like we'd never left. All of our loyal customers were either inside, waiting for a service, or had our appointment books filled up for the next month. I knew a lot of them were there just trying to be nosy, but as long as they were spending money, I didn't give a damn.

"Ooooh, this my shit! Turn it up, Tyrese!" Niqua, one of my stylists, shouted, already starting to groove as the intro to SZA's song "Snooze" came through the speakers.

Doing as she said, Tyrese snatched up the remote and increased the volume, causing the whole shop to start vibing. I hummed along as I put barrel curls into my client's freshly done sew-in. The lyrics had my mind wandering to a time when I felt the exact same way. I'd done all those things for Tramel, and I was ready to do the same for Zaakir, but both of those niggas had been disappointments.

I quickly finished and combed through her silky tresses before spinning her chair around so she could see the finished product. Pride instantly swelled in my chest at the huge smile that spread across her face as she ran her fingers through her hair and pulled out her phone. "Okaaaaay, you did yo' big one on this, boo! I can't wait to swing this shit in hoe's faces!" she squealed, already tossing her head from side to side as she recorded herself.

"Period!" I flipped my own hair, looking into her camera and swiping across my neck.

We shared a laugh before she paid me and promised to return in a few weeks for a touch-up. Once she was up, my next client took her seat, and I began to braid her hair down. I was halfway done when the bell chimed, alerting us all of someone entering. My shoulders immediately grew tense upon seeing Rome. My eyes shot to Tyrese's, and his entire demeanor changed from overtly feminine to that of a street nigga ready to get down if need be. I gestured discreetly to let him know I was okay, and he relaxed slightly but kept a hard gaze on Rome.

"What's good, sis?" His phony ass spread his arms wide as he came further into the salon.

Where I used to be happy to see him, I felt nothing but irritation now, and I struggled to keep the disdain I felt in my heart off my face.

"Hey, bro, I'm glad you could make it," I gushed, accepting the hug he offered. All eyes were on us, so when his hands started roaming up my back, I quickly backed away. Despite feeling like his goofy ass was on one, I hid my discomfort with a smile. "Come on back to my office," I told him and motioned for Tyrese to come handle my client for me.

"After you." Rome folded one hand over the other in front of himself with a shrug. I didn't particularly want to walk ahead of him in my tight ass leggings after the way he'd just tried to feel me up, but instead of making it a big deal, I bit the bullet and headed on back. "So, what's up? What you been blowin' my phone up for?" he wasted no time asking as soon as my office door closed behind us.

I hadn't expected him to get right to the point, so I was immediately caught off guard, especially with him looking at me all suspiciously. The small recorder I had attached to my broach only added to my level of anxiety, but I knew I needed to keep my composure if this shit was going to work.

"I uhhh, I need to know what's your boy's end game?" I sighed and hoped my voice wasn't as shaky as I thought.

His forehead bunched. "End game?"

"You know what I'm talking about, Rome. He all but told me he was the one who got me shot, then my shop gets raided, and they find drugs? Is he intentionally trying to have me locked up just because I moved on? After everything I've done for him. Really?" I was supposed to be gathering some type of information for Detective Hill, enough to get me off the hook, but I couldn't help asking a few questions of my own. A part of me just had to know how Tramel could do something like that to me, of all people, after years of putting my wants and needs aside for him.

Rome chuckled, snapping me out of my thoughts. "I don't know what you talkin' 'bout, *sis*. Mel wouldn't do no shit like that... but I can't say I'd blame him if he did. You know better than anybody that loyalty supposed to be matched, not given to the next nigga just 'cause you fuckin' him." His words had more fire behind them than I would've expected, but the way niggas acted over their friends, I shouldn't have been surprised. He was clearly going to ride with Tramel no matter what, despite him calling me sis. *Niggas really wasn't shit.*

"You sound crazy as hell! He's jeopardizing all our freedom because I don't wanna be with him no more? That's the dumbest shit I ever heard. It don't even make sense for you to be willing to go along with that shit."

"How the fuck our freedom on the line 'cause they found drugs in yo' shit? In case you ain't hear me, I said he *wouldn't* do no shit like that. Hell, he can't do none of the shit you accusing him of from behind bars, genius. Did you consider it might be yo' new nigga setting you up? You ain't even known that A'santi nigga that long. How the fuck you figure this ain't his doing?" he quizzed, tilting his head at me.

I'd been trying to keep Zaakir's name out of this because I didn't want him on the police's radar, but judging from the look on Rome's face, he'd mentioned him on purpose. Obviously, he felt like he couldn't trust me and wasn't going to say anything that would incriminate him or Tramel. I quickly realized when he was touching my back, he was looking for wire with his sneaky ass, and I rolled my eyes inwardly. I'd told them that he wasn't a dummy, and now I could only hope that Detective Hill hadn't picked up on Zaakir's family name and tried to rope them into this shit. That was the last thing I needed.

"I know because Tramel's dumb ass came up to the hospital and all but said he was gon' do this shit! Are you fuckin' listenin'?" I snapped with my nose turned up. "You're literally out here ridin' for his police ass, and who's to say he won't turn on you just like he did with me?"

"'Cause he won't—" he shot back, catching himself before he could say too much. His lips spread into a smirk, and he wagged a finger at me. "You're smart, but if you knew half as much as you thought you did, you'd gone 'head and accept yo' fate. Get a good lawyer and stop tryna drag me and Tramel into yo' shit." With that final warning, he left the same way he'd come, leaving my door wide open.

"Shit!"

Snatching off the ugly ass broach, I tossed it in my desk and dropped onto my swivel chair before rubbing my suddenly throbbing temples. It felt like I'd missed my chance with him. No way was he going to meet up with me again, considering he was already suspicious. If I tried to reach out again, I had no doubt he'd be ready to kill me this time. Then again, I saw a sliver of uncertainty when I mentioned Tramel turning on him, so maybe there was still a chance. I just needed to give him a reason to believe that Tramel wasn't as loyal as he made himself out to be, but that would be the hard part.

"Biiiitch, I take it things didn't go well." Tyrese's voice was full of concern, but I didn't lift my head to see the matching look of pity on his face.

"Nope."

"Well, I could've told you that. For one, you're either hot as hell since you just got out or working with the police since you just got out. Ain't no real street nigga gon' fuck with you under those circumstances. What?" He had the nerve to shrug when I looked up at him like he didn't know he was stating the obvious.

"I had to at least try, or my ass gon' be in prison tryna fight butch hoes up off me." I shuddered with my face balled up.

"You're so damn dramatic. You worried about somebody takin' it when you gon' fuck around and be throwin' that pussy around to whoever gon' catch it in there with how many years they're tryna give us. I know I am," he said, poking his ass out with his lips puckered. Despite the seriousness of the situation, I couldn't help but laugh.

"You make me sick! Can yo' ass just be serious for once? We need to figure this shit out."

"I mean, you could always call Zaaaaakiiiiir. Repent yo' sins and ask for—"

"I ain't callin' that nigga!" I grit, irritated that he was even bringing him up. Regardless of me telling him not to, Tyrese continued to mention him, and it bothered me for more than a couple reasons. I could deny my feelings and talk shit until I was blue in the face, but the truth was, I missed his black ass much more than I cared to admit.

"Okay, okay. I was just tryna help—"

"Well, if Zaakir is the only suggestion, keep it. I'll figure something out," I grumbled, waving him off and snatching up the papers on my desk to distract myself. I was happy when after a few seconds, his lanky ass switched out, leaving me to my thoughts. It was time to put another plan in motion.

ZAAKIR

I fell back against the couch in VIP and took another swig from my bottle as the stripper in front of me made her ass jiggle. As hard as she was going, she still couldn't hold my attention. I was too busy scrolling through Sevyn's social media on some stalker shit. Most women would've been posting subliminals and song lyrics after a breakup, but not her ass. The fact that she was at work promoting her skills instead of shaking her ass in somebody club should've made me feel better, but it didn't. Not even sliding in new pussy was helping to keep her mean ass off my mind, and since Shai was still out the way and not answering nobody's calls, I was on my own. I considered just reaching out to Sevyn, but it had been so long, there was no telling how she'd react. And if she got disrespectful, then I was gonna get disrespectful, and we'd be right back where we started.

"Damn, is you gon' throw some money or something? This ain't no free dance, nigga!"

I tore my eyes away from my screen to see the stripper mugging me with her hands on her thick hips. My face instantly balled up from the way she was coming at me, and I resisted the urge to choke her ass.

"Fuck you think you talkin' to? Maybe if yo' thumb lookin'

ass was paying more attention to dancin' instead of worrying about what I'm doin', then I would be throwing something!" I huffed, shooing her off. "Get yo' ass on! Ain't nobody called you over here anyway!"

"Not until you pay me for that dance! I been over here twenty minutes! I could've made at least a hundred dollars by now!" She went off, rolling her neck as she lied through her crooked ass teeth.

Snorting, I pulled a couple bills from my pocket and balled them up before tossing them in her direction. One hit her forehead, while the other hit her chest. She gasped dramatically but still bent to pick them up. Her face twisted up even more, realizing that I'd only given her twenty dollars.

"You an asshole, Zaakir!" she snapped, stuffing the money into her G-string before switching away.

That was her best bet, though, because I would've snatched that shit right back. I didn't even know why she'd slithered herself into my section anyway when it should've been obvious I was on some solo dolo shit. As soon as she was gone, my attention went back to my phone screen, and I wanted to go curse her simple ass out. Fucking around with her, I'd accidentally liked Sevyn's picture. It was an off-guard of her and some little girl whose hair she'd just braided. She looked pretty as hell with her hair pulled to the side in a lazy ponytail and barely there makeup. My finger hovered, ready to take my like back, but it was too late. She'd still see that I'd been on her page anyway.

Shaking my head, I exited the app and focused on the main stage, where two bitches were putting on a show that instantly wiped out any thoughts I had of Sevyn. They were basically fucking up there, and my dick came alive watching them kissing as they grinded against each other. I wasted no time waving over one of the bottle girls. I slipped her a couple bills to relay a message for me, and she happily ran off to do so.

The girls were just coming off the stage when she reached them, and judging from the way they were looking at me, I already knew they were down for whatever. Giving them a head nod, I finished my bottle and got ready to take them to the hotel. If two pussies couldn't evict Sevyn's ass from my mind, I didn't know what would.

An hour later, I watched them doing the exact same shit on the hotel bed that they'd been doing on stage, but this time, my dick was unmoved. No matter how much I tried to direct them, my joint was still deflated as fuck, just resting against my leg. I'd even set my drink aside, thinking maybe I'd had too much.

"Damn, Daddy, you don't wanna join us?" The one named Candy lifted her head from between Caramel's thighs and pouted at me. "I'm tryna feel that big muthafucka in my stomach." She moaned, continuing her assault on Caramel with her fingers.

"Why don't you feel it in yo' throat first?" I squeezed my dick, already feeling it stiffen a little.

Her eyes lit up, and she didn't hesitate to disengage from Caramel, licking her juices from her fingers as she crawled over to me. She gobbled me right up, and the wetter her mouth became, the harder my dick got until it was stretching her jaws to capacity. The sight was enough to have me shooting off early, and I grinned inwardly. For a minute, I thought my shit was broke, but I was happy as fuck to know it wasn't.

"Daaaaamn, just like that," I hissed, unable to close my mouth as I watched her make my dick disappear down her throat.

"Let me taste!" Caramel appeared out of nowhere on her hands and knees.

They went back and forth, sharing like it was a popsicle they were trying to keep from melting on a hot summer day. Real shit, if I'd been standing, my knees would've buckled with the way they were milking me. Before I knew it, I was shooting off, and they both fought to be the one who caught it.

"Argghhhh!" I growled as my stomach caved in. I felt like I'd never busted a nut before, and I grinned, seeing that despite my release, my dick was still slightly hard. It continued to grow with the added sensation of both girls still licking and slurping me up.

"Hell yeah! A nigga back!" I couldn't help cheering after that scare, causing Candy and Caramel to giggle. Unfazed. I nodded toward the bed, ready to do some damage. "Gone 'head get up there and put them asses in the air."

The next morning I woke up in my own bed with my balls drained and a big ass smile on my face. It grew even wider seeing Shai's name flashing across my phone screen. That nigga told me where he was going, but I hadn't spoken to him since then. After the shit his pops was on and then finding out Aunty was still fucking around with that nigga, I could understand him wanting to get away. Shit, even my pops was feeling some type of way about that little development. He'd wanted to kick Giorgio's ass, and I would've helped him if we weren't in front of the police station.

"Nigga, tell me yo' ass finally back. I'm tired of Casa and yo' mama pressing me like I got control over you or some shit," I teased, only half joking.

Our parents had been getting on my fucking nerves worrying about his ass, more so Casa than Queen, and that was only 'cause he knew his sister was going through it. If I was smart, I would've taken my ass with him or, at the very least, gone out to Miami for some R and R my damn self.

He chuckled, sounding much more at peace than he had the last time I'd spoken to him. Although I stayed talking shit, I was happy for him. Having a pops who would put you through some shit like a fake arrest was crazy as hell, and then to find out he messing with his mama after leaving her to raise him alone? It was some straight up Jerry Springer shit, but the illegal version.

"Yeah, I'm just now touchin' down. You ain't have to answer them muhfuckas tho... shit, I didn't."

"That's easy for yo' ass to say when you was damn near two thousand miles away from here. All you had to do was tap the screen to avoid their asses, but you know neither of them got a problem pulling up. Shit, I'm surprised Queen ass ain't catch a flight and come get you her damn self."

"Naw, she too busy sneaking around with Gio's ass to do all that," he grumbled absentmindedly.

"Ayite, bro, I know you in yo' feelings and shit, but I ain't tryna think about Aunty and Gio's pasty ass creepin'."

"I wasn't even goin' there. Man, yo' ass tweakin' right now!" He fumed, and I could tell his face was bright red without even seeing him.

"You sound goofy as hell. Fuck else you thought they was sneaking around doin'? Baking and shit?" I cackled. "Nigga, yo' white side slippin' out. You better tighten up!"

"Man, fuck you!"

I was still laughing when the phone beeped, indicating that he'd hung up on me, but I was used to him throwing tantrums whenever I talked shit about his white side. He'd get over it. Letting out a yawn, I stretched and climbed out of bed to handle my hygiene so I could get my day started. If Shai was back, Casa was definitely going to call us over there. I'd barely gotten out of the shower when my phone went off, and I instantly squinted, seeing the unsaved number on the screen. My first instinct was to not answer that shit, but instead of listening to my first mind, I pressed accept.

"Yoo!" I greeted, setting the phone on the sink and putting it on speaker so I could brush my teeth.

"Hello? Zaaaaakiiiiir!"

I froze in the middle of putting toothpaste on my toothbrush when I heard Tyrese's voice. It didn't take a rocket scientist to figure he got my number from Sevyn's weird ass, but the question was, why the fuck was he calling me? I hadn't talked to that nigga since Sevyn was in the hospital. Plus, the way he got ghost along with her other stylists after the raid had me suspicious as fuck. I'd seen him in pictures with Sevyn on her page while I was snooping, so I knew they were back cool, but that didn't mean I was comfortable with his ass hitting my line.

Seconds passed while I stood silently, trying to think of what he could possibly want. "Hello?"

"Yeah, what's up?" I said, finally lining my toothbrush and hitting it with some water. He sighed in relief and mumbled "Thank God" under his breath, but I still heard his extra ass.

"Look, I don't got a lot of time before Sevyn comes back. I know y'all call yourselves not fucking with each other right now, but regardless of how in denial y'all are, I know both y'all miss each other and—"

"Aye, man, get to the fuckin' point," I interrupted, spitting out a mouthful of toothpaste.

"Tuh! Nigga, I will if you let me finish!" His tone dripped with attitude, and I had to resume my brushing to keep from cursing him the fuck out. I bucked my eyes like he could see me as I waited for his extra ass to continue. "Like I was saying, I know y'all miss each other but are just too stubborn to admit it—"

"You don't know shit," I quickly denied, making him suck his teeth.

"Boy, please, you was just on her IG, liking a pic from last week when I know she been posting every day. That tells me you been on her page in your feelings, sooo...."

"That was an accident!"

"Whatever helps you sleep at night, Zaaaaaakiiiiir, but I didn't call to argue with you. Sevyn's in trouble, and she's tryna handle it herself, but she's in over her head with this one. That bitch ass nigga Tramel and his little sidekick gon' have us all behind bars and—"

"I ain't got shit to do with anything Sevyn and her *husband* got goin' on. Ain't none of that shit my business." My face tightened at the mention of her and that nigga in the same sentence. I still planned to kill his ass, but that didn't have shit to do with Sevyn. I wanted that nigga for taking my baby's life, and I was going to make sure I made him suffer.

"You know what? Fine, Zaaakiiiir! You wanna let yo' pride stop you from helping the woman you love, by all means, do that, but I hope you can live with yourself—matter fact, what am I even saying? Of course, your selfish ass can! The way y'all niggas can scream loyalty but turn yo' back on a muthafucka is crazy as hell! I was really out here rooting for you, but it's definitely fuck yo' black ass now!" he snapped and hung up in my face before I could even get a word in.

In five minutes, Tyrese had asked for my help then turned around and put me in my place. I tried to tell myself his words didn't bother me, but that shit plagued me the entire time I finished getting ready for the day. By the time I left the house, I'd made up my mind to pop up on Sevyn to find out what the fuck was going on.

SEVYN

I pulled up into my garage after a long ass day and sighed
heavily. On one hand, I was relieved to have my shop and
home back, but on the other, I was more than a little over-
whelmed by everything on my plate. Although I was putting on a
big front for Tyrese and my other stylists like I had shit under
control, I was having a meltdown inside, which was why I was
about to crack open a bottle and drown my sorrows in the
bottom of that motherfucker.

After grabbing all my things, I locked up my car and switched
inside, turning on lights as I entered. The sound of my phone
going off had me hurrying to dig it out of my purse. I wasn't at all
surprised to see Tyrese's name on my screen since he'd been making
it his business to ensure I made it to my car and then calling me
when I got home. This had become our nightly routine, and
although his concern was unnecessary, I appreciated the gesture.

"Hey, Ty," I dragged, unable to stop myself from smiling.

"Nah, uh, heffa! Don't be tryna act like I'm bothering you!"

Giggling, I pulled my bottle out and went to grab a glass while
he continued to go off. "Ain't shit funny. I'm tryna check on yo'
baldheaded ass and be a good friend, and look at how you do me!"

"Daaaamn, bitch, you goin' off, and I ain't even said shit!" I feigned innocence, but I was sure the laughter was still evident in my voice.

"You ain't have to say nothin'. I know from the way you answered that you was irritated. Now you over there laughin' like a hyena. You ain't slick."

"That's 'cause I ain't tryna be slick. You just funny as hell."

"Whatever! Is you in the house yet, while you talkin' shit?" His mad ass sucked his teeth.

"Yes, daddy, I'm home safe and sound with all the doors locked." My voice was sugary sweet, knowing my sarcasm would only piss him off more.

Instead of responding, he hung up on me. I snickered as I pulled up our text thread and sent him a kissing emoji. Of course, his butt-hurt ass sent back a middle finger, and I made a mental note to bring him breakfast and a coffee in the morning to make up for my teasing. I was playing around, but the truth was, Tyrese had been helping me keep my head above water, especially since I wasn't trying to burden Zuri with my bullshit, and I was extremely grateful.

Leaving my purse on the island, I carried my half-empty glass and the whole bottle with me so I could run a nice bath. The plan was to soak and blast some music until I got tipsy enough to rest my mind, but the second I passed my dining room, I had to back-track. Seeing the dark frame sitting at the head of the table had a scream bubbling up in my throat, and I wanted to kick my own ass for leaving my purse in the kitchen.

"Sevyn, chill, man. It's just me."

A mixture of emotions shot through me when I heard Zaakir's voice. It had been weeks, and I'd convinced myself that I didn't want to see him again, but the way my heart was pounding said otherwise. Frozen, I swallowed the lump in my throat, scared to step any closer to him.

"What the fuck you doin'? Cut the damn light on and sit yo'

drunk ass down!" he snapped, and I immediately remembered why it had been so long since we'd spoken.

Sucking my teeth, I flipped the light on, getting even more irritated by how good he looked. As usual, he was decked out in designer and shining from his ears, neck, and wrists with a fresh cut that had his waves on swim.

"How the hell you get in here?" My tone was clipped when I finally found my voice.

It dawned on me that he could've found out about my involvement with the police and came to kill me. The shit certainly made sense after not hearing from him, just for his ass to suddenly pop up. I couldn't help looking for a quick exit or a weapon I could use just in case. My gaze landed on the silver candelabras that rested in the center of the table. I was still considering if I could reach it before his crazy ass pulled his gun when his gritty voice broke through my thoughts.

"Sit," he repeated, mugging me like he wasn't the one who broke into my house.

Still, instead of getting smart like I wanted to, I dropped into the chair closest to me, which happened to be at the opposite end of the table. We sat staring at each other in silence for I don't know how long before I lifted my glass with a sigh.

"I really don't have the time or mental capacity to play with yo' ass right now, Zaakir. So, can you please just tell me what the fuck you're doin' here, so I can finish my bottle in peace?" I was proud of myself for how confident that came out when I was shook on the inside.

Unfazed, Zaakir took his time responding. His face remained neutral, and I couldn't help squirming under his scrutinizing gaze. "What you got goin' on, Sev?" He squinted like he could see right through my tough act, and I looked away.

Don't panic, bitch! He doesn't know anything! I tried to hype myself up mentally, but it did nothing to help my nerves. If anything, his question only worried me more. It was vague, and the lack of emotion on his face had me on edge.

"I really don't know what you're talkin' about. You gon' have to be more specific than that," I said, locking eyes with him once again.

I wasn't about to admit to shit, but I was hoping he'd give me something to let me know exactly what *he* thought I had going on. For all I knew, Zaakir's crazy ass could've been talking about another nigga, even though he was the reason behind our breakup. That thought alone had me relaxing just a little.

Sighing in exasperation, he leaned forward and clasped his hands together. "I'm talkin' about Tyrese's aggy ass callin' me, saying you in trouble and that you need help. Then I get here, and you takin' a bottle to the head and complainin' about yo' damn mental capacity and shit. So, I'm askin' what the fuck you got going on?"

I ran my tongue along my teeth and chuckled bitterly. I'd specifically told Tyrese that I didn't want to rope Zaakir into this shit, and he'd gone behind my back to call him since I wouldn't. My leg shook beneath the table, and I drained my glass to stall. Tyrese running his mouth had put me in a tight spot because lying was the reason behind our falling out in the first place. While I had been trying to prep myself for a life without Zaakir, I couldn't deny that a small part of me still held out hope for us, but I was sure if I lied to him again, there would definitely be no chance of reconciliation. Then again, telling him I was fucking with the police in any capacity could also put a nail in the coffin of our relationship.

I poured another glass while I contemplated my next move. Zaakir watched me closely the whole time, but the minute I swallowed it all down and tried to pour another, his patience ran out. He smacked his lips and pushed away from the table, making a loud ass noise as the chair scraped my damn hardwood floor.

"Okay!" I shouted at his back before I could change my mind. "A stipulation of my release is turning on Tramel! They want me to get his connect." My tone lowered considerably, seeing the way he stiffened, and tears suddenly burned my eyes. Besides being on the brink of death, I didn't know why I was about to cry all of a sudden.

He turned around slowly, his face twisted in a mixture of disbelief and disgust. I shrunk under his glare, feeling like a child about to be reprimanded. Before I knew it, he'd crossed the room and had yanked me up by my shirt.

"The fuck you mean! You workin' with the Feds now? Is my name mixed up in this shit? You tryna give them niggas a two for one?" he barked, shaking me like a ragdoll, and pain immediately shot through my body.

"What? No!" I was a blubbering mess, unable to stop the tears that had now spilled onto my face. "I swear, I wouldn't do that!"

"What the fuck, bro!" He growled and released me with a shove that had me landing right back in my chair as I cried hysterically.

I hopped up, grabbing at his shirt to stop him from backing away. "I swear, I've been trying to keep you out of this! I never mentioned your name! They only want Tramel and his people!"

"How I'm sposed to trust that, Sevyn? Yo' ass lie so much; I wouldn't be surprised if this whole shit was a setup. Got Tyrese ass hittin' me up and shit! Man, what the fuck!" I jumped as he punched the wall, leaving a hole before beginning to pace. He was mumbling under his breath as he pulled out his phone.

Despite his reaction, I continued to plead with him. "Baby, I swear I wouldn't. Tyrese called you to help get me out of this, not set you up! I know it probably looks bad, but—"

"It looks bad?" He scoffed, setting his steely glare my way. His question was rhetorical, but I still nodded anyway.

"Yes, but I'm telling you, this doesn't have shit to do with you! I don't fuck with the police just like you don't, but if getting justice means setting that nigga up, then so what? Don't forget that he originally started this police shit! He put a hit out on me and killed our baby, and when that didn't work, he had Rome plant drugs in my shop! You're mad at me when I don't say shit, and now you're mad that I am! Make up your fuckin' mind! It ain't like that nigga followed code, so why the fuck should I?"

My own anger boiled over just thinking about the shit Tramel had done, yet I had to explain my reasoning for giving his stupid ass a dose of his own medicine. I completely understood niggas and their issues with the police, but working with them was the only card I had to play.

He stared at me in silence, and I glared right back, chest still heaving. "Let me get the fuck up outta here before I kill yo' stupid ass," he said after a few tense seconds had passed.

"Fuck you, Zaakir!"

"Fuck me?"

"Yeah, fuck you! You don't have the right to judge shit I do! You abandoned me when I needed you most, so I did what I had to do! It wasn't like yo' black ass was stepping up!"

"Nah, when you needed me the most, I gave yo' ungrateful ass a piece of me!" he slowly trod over, only stopping when he was so close our noses almost touched. "When you needed me, I was there every-fuckin-day! That nigga got you so fucked up in the head that you can't even tell when a muthafucka really love you!" he fumed, immediately taking all the fight out of me.

We both seemed to be stunned by the admission since Zaakir had never said those words before. Although it was indirect, I still knew exactly what he meant. I don't know who leaned in first, but one minute, we were glaring at each other, and the next, our bodies were connected as his lips met mine.

ZAAKIR

I lay next to a sleeping Sevyn, confused as fuck. How the hell we'd gone from screaming at each other to fucking was a mystery to me, but I couldn't deny it was the best sex I'd ever had with her conniving ass. I was out here bad, doing shit I would've never done under normal circumstances. I'd slipped up and basically said I loved her, then took the pussy after finding out she was a damn informant. Casa would fucking disown my black ass if he knew. Shit, Shai probably would too, and he was the most soft-hearted nigga I knew when it came to women.

Then again, this was right up my cousin's alley. My brows bunched at the thought of me acting like that nigga, and I realized it was too late. I'd already fallen into the deep end when it came to Sevyn. She'd already carried my baby, gotten part of my liver, and now I was turning a blind eye to her fucking with the police. Fuck my player's card; I was gon' mess around and lose my gangster status behind this shit. She let out a little moan in her sleep, snuggling closer. Despite the thoughts running through my mind, my first instinct was to wrap my arm around her. *Shit!*

Being around Sevyn always had a way of making me switch up, and I needed to get the fuck from by her janky ass. Taking my time, I slid out of her reach, pausing every few seconds so I didn't disturb her until I was on the edge of the bed. Once I was no longer under her, I released the breath I was holding and went in search of my phone.

Before I'd gotten sidetracked, I'd been trying to call my pops, but his ass wasn't picking up, which was probably for the best. Last time I went to him for advice, he talked all kinds of shit and ended up being the reason Sevyn left my crib in the first place. Besides that, he would be trying to put a bullet in her head. I couldn't really go to Shai's ass either because there was no telling what type of advice he would give me. This was going to require a much smoother hand, and I knew just the person to go to.

I found my phone still in the dining room and shot a quick text to Queen, letting her know I needed to stop by the next day. As expected, she hit me right back, unfazed by the late hour when it came to messages from me or Shai. Once that was done, I called up Campbell. Since he was on retainer, he answered, voice groggy as fuck from sleep.

"Wake yo' bitch ass up, nigga!" I hissed, trying to keep my voice down just in case Sevyn woke up.

"Zaakir?" he sounded puzzled. "What's going on?"

"I need some info on yo' boy Brian." I got right to the point, and the line fell silent. He knew better than anybody what I meant, so I was sure his heart rate sped up.

"W-why? What happened?"

"Since yo' ass couldn't come up with a better solution for my girl than for her to turn herself in, she went to that nigga, and he let them convince her to become a fuckin' informant! Now I kinda feel like you're partly to blame for this, but I'm gon' give you a chance to turn this shit around. I can't say the same for that nigga, though." I allowed my words to sink in, hoping he understood the same shit that was going to happen to Brian would happen to him if he fumbled this case like that nigga did.

"I can't—"

I shook my head with a bitter chuckle. Obviously, he wasn't getting it despite the keywords I'd thrown around, but he was going to. "Listen, Campbell, all you need to say is, 'Yes sir, I'll get right on it.' All that other shit ain't necessary." My tone was light, like I wasn't threatening him, and after a few seconds of silence, he seemed to get the picture. I heard him swallow hard before telling me everything he knew about Brian Silver, just like I knew he would.

I left Sevyn's crib before she woke up and before the sun rose, already knowing that she was going to be pissed. After the way she had completely cut me off the last time, I wasn't expecting a call or shit from her, but I fully intended to get back up with her ass once I tied up a few loose strings. I headed home to shower and throw on some clothes before heading to Queen's crib. Seeing Giorgio's car in her driveway was some shit I wasn't expecting after what happened with him, but I figured his connections could come in handy too. I was still going to tell my cousin about that shit, though, just not right away.

I headed to the door, eying the two men sitting in the car on security duty. They were the same ones who were with him at the police station, so I made sure to mug them as I walked by. When I made it to her stoop and hit the bell, I wasn't surprised when her punctual ass opened it right up like she had been standing there waiting for me.

"What took you so long?" she fussed, ushering me inside.

"My bad, Aunty. I had to go change clothes." Shrugging, I bent down to give her a hug and kiss on her cheek.

"Mmmhmm."

She gave me a knowing look and locked up before following me deeper inside. The smell of breakfast had me heading toward the kitchen, and I wasn't disappointed when I saw the spread she had set up. "Daaaamn, Aunty, you hooked it up!" I pushed up the sleeves of my hoodie, and she rubbed the back of her neck with one of those girlish smiles.

"Yeah, I figured you'd be hungry, but you better go wash your hands before you touch anything." She was quick to stop me from dropping into a seat, and I begrudgingly went to the hall bathroom to do what she said.

By the time I made it back, my face balled up at the sight of Giorgio sitting at the head of the table. He looked comfortable as hell, further proving that he'd been kicking it with Queen on the low for a minute. And judging by the Gucci slippers on his feet, he had personal shit there, too. I eyed him as I entered, giving him a short nod that he returned before taking a seat across from him. His plate was already piled high with everything she'd cooked, and I started doing the same.

Queen shuffled back into the room and cleared her throat as she sat down, prompting him to crack his neck uncomfortably before speaking. "I, uh... I wanted to apologize about what happened last week. Like I said, it was a necessary reassurance, and now that it's out of the way, you nor Shai won't have to worry about any more issues like that again," he said, cutting his eyes at Queen as if for approval as she casually sipped her coffee.

I choked down a laugh. She had his white ass wrapped around her finger, and just from the look on his face, I knew he'd be willing to do whatever she wanted.

"I get it." I shrugged, grinning when I saw his body sag with relief. "I don't know what Shai gon' do, but I ain't trippin'. I might need a favor to fully put this behind us, though."

His brows shot up at the request, and he looked at Queen again. "What kind of *favor*?"

I finished buttering my pancakes as I tried to think of how to word this shit and eventually said fuck it. Whatever I requested just needed to be approved by Queen for him to go along with it, so instead of telling him, I turned to her.

"My girl got involved in some shit with her uh... husband." It pained me to say, but I managed to get it out. "That nigga is the one who shot her and set her up by planting some drugs in her shop—"

"Wait, the one that's in prison?" Queen's nose turned up in confusion.

"Yeah. His ass is way more connected than I gave him credit for. So much so that the police tryna get her to flip on that nigga." I followed up with a grave look, and they both understood immediately.

Queen's eyes bucked, and she gasped while Giorgio squinted across the table at me. "Like an informant?" He asked for clarification, and I nodded. Silence fell over the table as they shared a look before he spoke again. "What do you think I can do for you, Zaakir?"

"I need her off their radar completely. No CI shit, none of that. Can yo' boys at the police department make that happen?" I put it all on the table, well, some of it, anyway.

I wasn't about to admit that Sevyn was fully involved in that nigga's business. Queen loved the fuck out of me and Shai, but she was a girl's girl at heart, and knowing Tramel's ass had done Sevyn dirty would undoubtedly have her on our side.

He appeared to be considering whether my request was feasible while I waited impatiently. Of course, I was hoping they could help since an inside job would be the easiest method, but I wasn't opposed to handling shit my own way.

"I'll make some calls and see what I can do, but it'll take some time. Do you think she can stall the investigation for a while until we figure this thing out?" My forehead creased as I contemplated.

To be honest, I didn't know shit about informants or how long the police allowed them to take while getting evidence. The whole shit was stupid to me, anyway, considering the nigga they were after was locked the fuck up. I didn't even know any plug that would've still been willing to serve his ass.

"I don't know, but I gotta make a visit to the lawyer who set this shit up, so I'm sure I can get the answer to that for you."

"Okay, good. You do that, and I'll see what I can find out on my end and get back to you."

Queen released a heavy sigh and then smiled brightly. "Okay, now that that's handled, can we eat?" As bad as I wanted to actually sit and enjoy my food, I knew I needed to get up with Brian ASAP so Giorgio could do his thing.

I grabbed my plate and shoveled some eggs into my mouth as I came around to her side. "I'ma have to take a raincheck, Aunty, but this shit hittin'. You mind if I take it with me?" I asked, giving her a quick one-armed hug as she sputtered.

"Uh-boy! You better bring my damn plate back! That's my good China!" she shouted at my back since I was already heading down the hall. I was going to finish my food in the car on the way to Brian's crib.

SEVYN

It had been a week since I'd woken up to an empty bed, and I felt played as fuck. I couldn't believe I'd let that nigga trick me out some pussy, just to pull another disappearing act, this time worse than the last. It definitely had me feeling more hurt than last time. I'd put my pride to the side and told him the whole truth, just for him to hit me with the same move. To be completely honest, my feelings were more hurt than anything, but at least he hadn't killed me.

"Girl, you need to stop moping around here. You're bringing the vibe down." Tyrese huffed, switching past where I sat on his couch and plopping down next to me.

I was still very much pissed at him for setting me up the way he had, but I knew his heart was in the right place, so I hadn't been too hard on him. Rolling my eyes, I tucked my feet beneath me, getting even more comfortable because I wasn't going anywhere until it was time for me to meet Zuri for dinner. She'd come back from her little baecation, but I wanted to let her get settled in and back to her regular schedule before getting together. Plus, I wanted to feel her out a little to make sure Zaakir hadn't gone running his mouth to Shai.

"Don't start with me. If it wasn't for you mindin' *my* business, I wouldn't be fuckin' up your vibe." I waved him off and took another sip of my margarita.

"I mean, look on the bright side. At least all he did was drop off some dick." He shrugged, unbothered. "He could've dropped you off on God's doorstep, and you wouldn't be over here drinking up my good Patrón." He had the nerve to bow his head and press his hands together like he was praying.

Despite my mood, I couldn't help flashing back to the way Zaakir had fucked me. Angry sex with him had to be the best I'd ever had with him or anybody else. I shuddered just thinking about it and quickly tried to play it off when I saw Tyrese's eyes on me.

"Uhhnhuh! You can thank me for that!"

"Shut up!" I sneered, throwing one of his decorative pillows at him. "Matter fact, let me get up outta here before I'm late." I stood and set my glass on the coffee table. It was almost time for me to meet up with Zuri anyway.

"Don't nobody care, hoe. My man bouta come over here anyway."

That only had me raising my middle finger before speeding even faster to gather my things and go. My mind was already on my next drink, and I wasn't ashamed to say that's how I'd been coping as of late. I stuck my tongue out at him as I made it to the door and swung it open to see a short, stocky ass nigga on the other side.

Tyrese hopped up quickly to greet him as I slipped past, pulling my coat tighter around me. The way that cold ass air hit me had me less worried about the mini thug Tyrese was trying to entertain and more worried about making it to my car before I froze to death. I fished around in my purse for my keys as I speed walked, only getting a full grasp on them once I was within a foot of my car.

"Mrs. Ellis—"

"Ahhhhh!" my heart damn near jumped out of my chest at the deep ass voice just randomly coming out of the dark. It only took me a second to register that it was Detective Hill's aggra-vating ass, and once I did, I immediately sucked my teeth. "What the fuck you sneakin' up on me for?" I shouted, looking around to make sure nobody saw me talking to him, even though Tyrese stayed in a fairly lowkey neighborhood.

"Sorry, I didn't mean to scare you." He raised his hands in front of him as if trying to put me at ease, but that did little to calm my racing heart.

"So, why you just pop up in the dark, calling my name and shit?" Reaching down, I retrieved my keys that I'd dropped and turned my back on him to open the door.

I wasn't interested in shit his ass had to say, considering the shit they'd gotten me into, and I made a mental note to call Brian. There had to be something he could do to get them to back off before they got me killed.

"May I?" He gestured toward the car.

I narrowed my eyes at him for a few seconds and then nodded, begrudgingly tapping the lock so he could get in. We both fell into the seats at the same time, and he got right to it. "Have you told anybody about your CI status?"

His inquiry had my brows raising in both question and alarm. I immediately had to wonder what the fuck Zaakir had done to make his ass ask me something like that.

I was already shaking my head before my lips moved, and I prayed it didn't make me look suspicious. "No. Why the fuck would I do some shit like that? Do I look like I wanna die or something? Who the hell would I even tell, anyway?"

He didn't respond right away; he only stared at me long and hard as if trying to see through my act. His silence made me even more uncomfortable, and I avoided his eyes, cursing under my breath when I realized how suspicious that probably looked.

Even if his ass was onto me, he played it off well, sighing before finally speaking. "Your lawyer was found dead in his home last night from what appears to be a home invasion gone wrong."

Now that was something I wasn't expecting to hear come out

of his mouth, and I sucked in a sharp breath at the news. I hadn't known Brian for long, but the few times I'd met with him, he seemed genuine and seemed to have my best interest at heart. It wasn't lost on me that he mentioned it appeared to be a home invasion as if they suspected something else had happened. I couldn't imagine why anybody would want him dead, but his status as a criminal defense lawyer could've very well played a role. So, I was even more confused about why they automatically assumed I was the reason, which is what I asked him.

"Jerome Smith is missing, and we have reason to believe he has been since you met with him at your shop," he hinted, wide-eyed the way cops do.

"Why the fuck would I tell someone as dangerous as Rome that I'm working to take him and his best friend down? And if I did tell him, why would he kill my damn lawyer and not me? Like, where is your reasoning?" I couldn't help asking.

I didn't know if he was just fucking with me or if his ass was just cynical by nature. Judging from his profession, I had to assume the latter. It was either that, or he was just a flaming idiot, which I could also assume was true.

His eye twitched as he stared at me, an unamused look covering his face. "I honestly don't know, but what I do know is that there's something fishy going on with this whole case, and if I find out you have anything to do with it, I'm gonna have your ass charged with everything from that kilo I found in your shop to accessory to murder. You're already on borrowed time, and with Rome missing, there won't be much use for you. Remember that," he threatened, leaving me too stunned to even speak.

I watched him exit my car with my mouth dropped open, wondering what the fuck had just happened.

SHAI

I finished up the paperwork I'd been filling out and closed the folder with a sigh. I'd been at Suave for hours, trying to play catch up, which I'd been doing for the last week. It seemed like the whole time I'd been gone, shit had been going downhill. Two of my line cooks had quit, one of the hostesses had broken her leg, and we were short on a lot of our normal food and drinks. I couldn't really blame Carla because she'd stepped in and was helping on the floor so much that she wasn't able to put in orders or set up interviews in my absence. Shit, even with me back, I was having a hard time finding replacements for my staff. So, just like her, I had been trying to pick up the slack, which meant a lot of extra hours, way more than I was used to doing.

Stretching, I checked the time on my phone. It was quickly approaching ten at night, and I knew if I didn't leave right then, I'd fuck around and not make it home in time to catch Zuri. We were nearing the home stretch, and SJ had her tired as fuck. She was beginning to fall asleep earlier every night, and a few times, her ass had even fallen asleep at the dinner table. If the doctor hadn't said that it was normal considering what all she did in a day, I would've thought she'd developed narcolepsy or some shit.

Thankfully, it would be over soon, though. She'd already

picked out the home she liked the most out of the five my real estate agent had shown us and was actively working with an interior designer. Since I'd been stuck at work, she kept me updated with pictures and made sure to ask my opinion on which colors I liked best, even though I didn't give a damn about any of that shit. As long as Zuri was happy and got everything she wanted, she could make all the decisions.

My phone ringing brought me out of my thoughts, and I sighed, seeing Casa's name. He really hadn't been on me too hard about the business, and I was grateful that he was stepping in for me while I got the restaurant together, but him calling this late couldn't have been a good thing. Still, I scooped up my phone and accepted the call before he could be sent to voicemail.

"What's up, Casa?" I tensed, hoping he wasn't trying to have me running around when all I wanted to do was climb in bed behind my woman.

"Get yo' ass over here to my house *now!*" was all he said before hanging up on me, and I sighed heavily.

The last thing I wanted to do was drive out to that nigga's crib, but obviously, whatever his issue was, it was serious. I quickly cleared my desk and stood, slipping on my suit jacket, and silently prayed that whatever he wanted didn't take long.

"Shai—oh, you're leaving already?" Carla appeared at my side as I stepped out. Her eyes showed her disappointment, but like always, I ignored the weird shit she was on.

"Yeah, I got an emergency. Is something wrong?" I quizzed, taking another step.

"Oh, no, I was just gonna let you know that everything's done, and the staff is all gone. So, it's just us...." Her voice lowered in what I assumed she thought was a sexy way, and she moved closer.

I didn't know what had gotten into her because she was so obvious when she tried to come on to me before. Frowning, I put another foot of distance between us and geared up to shut her thirsty ass down once again.

"Carla, I don't know what you think this is. I've told you on more than one occasion that I'm not interested, and more importantly, I have a woman. Now, if remaining professional is too much for you to handle, then I'll have to find somebody else who can." I made sure my tone was firm and my words were concise so there wasn't any room for her to misunderstand. This was the last chance I was going to give her ass before I fired her, and I was hoping she took heed.

"I-uhh... I'm so sorry. I didn't mean—"

"It's cool," I lied. "Just don't let it happen again, and make sure you lock up." I was already moving toward the door again, not wanting her to feel the need to say shit else to me.

It took me almost an hour to get to Casa's crib, and I almost didn't want to get out once I pulled up. That's how tired I was. After a few minutes, I finally sighed and climbed out. As usual, his ass opened the door before I could knock, and I shook my head at his paranoid ass.

"What's up, Unc?"

"Yeah, yeah, get yo' ass in here," he grumbled, stepping aside to let me in. I could already tell what type of time he was on from the drink in his hand, but I went ahead and walked further into the foyer. "Gone into my office. I'm right behind you." He sounded anything but happy to follow me in there, and when I finally made it to his office, I knew exactly why. Giorgio, Queen, and Zaakir all turned their heads in my direction once I entered, and I angrily balled my fists up.

"Fuck is this, an intervention or some shit?" I scoffed, refusing to step any further into the room.

"Man, get yo' ass in there," Casa voiced behind me with a shove. "I swear I'm starting to see what the fuck Zaakir goofy ass be talkin' 'bout with that light skin shit. Everything ain't about you, nigga." He talked shit as he came around and sat on the edge of his desk.

"Not too much on my baby!" my OG was quick to say, hopping out of her seat.

"Sit the fuck down, Queen! All y'all niggas really gettin' on my muthafuckin' nerves." He let out a bitter chuckle and shook his head. "All y'all out here going rogue got me fucked up! Did you know this nigga's bitch an informant?" he quizzed, pointing to Zaakir, and my forehead instantly bunched.

"Don't call her no bitch, man!"

"Boy, sit yo' tender dick ass down!" Casa thundered, standing to his feet and silencing Zaakir.

No lie, I was surprised as fuck. That nigga didn't even try to deny it, so I knew it was true. I jumped right in his face, yanking his little ass up out of his seat.

"That bitch investigatin' us, and you knew about this shit?"

He shoved me away with his face balled up. "She ain't a bitch, and they ain't on us. They on her bitch ass husband!" he fumed, sounding stupid as hell.

"How the fuck you know that, 'cause she told you?" I laughed sinisterly. "You be talkin' all that shit about me being soft, and yo' ass out here fuckin' the police!"

"Shiiiit, she's the police and the plug!" Casa cut in. "But that ain't all, Neph. This muthafucka done got tweedle dee and tweedle dumb involved, and then, this my favorite part. His ass done killed her lawyer!"

"First of all, don't be talkin' about me like I ain't standing right here, and you're damn right I helped. My nephew came to me 'cause he couldn't come to yo' judgmental ass!"

"Maaaan, shut up, Queen. You always tryna baby these niggas. *That's* why he came to you. You and this white muthafucka the only ones ready to condone this bullshit. He knew I'd have nipped this shit in the bud, starting with that big mouth ass hoe he fuckin'." He shrugged, moving to his chair and sitting down slowly. "Boom, problem solved."

"Ain't nobody gon' touch her! I keep tellin' you muthafuckas she ain't on us!"

Sucking my teeth, I moved from within arm's reach of that nigga before I fucked around and put my hands on his goofy ass.

Sevyn working with the police was the last thing I saw coming, and I couldn't help wondering if Zuri knew about this shit, considering how close they were. That opened up a whole other shit load of problems for me because loyalty was something I didn't play about. I was already in my head, analyzing everything as I moved across the room and posted up against the wall.

"It's really no reason for y'all to be doing all this. Gio and I looked into this thoroughly, and yes, Sevyn is an informant, but only to get her husband's plug." Queen attempted to reason with us. "Zaakir was outta order for killin' the lawyer, but I mean, after the type of deal he made for her, his ass should've died. He basically got that girl working to take down a huge crime boss with only the promise of possibly getting off. Ain't none of that shit on paper."

"So, fuckin' what? If her ass wasn't washing her husband's money, she wouldn't be in this shit. None of this got shit to do with us," Casa spewed.

"Fuck what you talkin' 'bout? If it got something to do with my girl, then it got something to do with me. Shai, you'd do the same thing for Zuri. And Casa, if my OG was alive, you'd definitely be standing ten toes down for her, right, wrong, or indifferent, and I wouldn't be able to do shit but respect it. So, y'all niggas gon' have to respect my shit." Zaakir stuck his chest out like he'd actually made a point, and to an extent, he had, but that didn't stop Casa and me from both bursting out laughing.

"Zuri or your mama wouldn't be married to another nigga, and I know my bitch wasn't gon' be striking up no deal with the police. I don't know about Zuri, but yo' mama was thorough."

"Sevyn thorough too, but that nigga tried to kill her then set her up to take the fall for his drugs! It's being loyal and being stupid, and I can't say I blame her for tryna save herself."

"Right, but didn't all this shit start because she was fuckin' yo' black ass?" Casa challenged, tilting his head. "Matter fact, don't even answer that. I'm not tryna go back and forth with you.

Our main focus needs to be covering yo' tracks and making sure we're not under investigation."

"That's what I've been trying to tell you. Yo' ass knows so much, but Gio already talked to his contacts, and nobody in this room is being investigated. Sevyn really is on the books to get her husband's connect, ol' dramatic ass nigga." Queen smacked her lips as she addressed her brother, and my eyes landed on Casa to see what he had to say about that.

"And they gave you some type of proof about this?" He turned to Giorgio, who tossed up his hands with a nod.

"I even got the emails to prove it."

Casa was silent for a few seconds as he mulled over the latest development in his case against Sevyn. He wasn't playing any games when it came to this situation, and I couldn't say I blamed him. But if my mama said some shit was true, then it was.

He stroked his beard and narrowed his eyes on Giorgio. "Send that to me, and in the meantime, don't you do shit else, nigga." His gaze shifted to Zaakir. "We may be in the clear now, but your ties to ol' girl could be the reason we end up on those pigs' radar."

Just looking at my cousin, I knew that nigga wasn't gonna listen to shit Unc was talking about. His face was all screwed up as he slouched down in the leather chair like a kid getting lectured. I wanted to speak on the shit but thought better of it. I was already stretched thin, but I'd have to make a special exception and add his ass to my list of responsibilities.

"Man, I hear you," he snapped after Casa repeated himself.

"Nigga, don't get all pissy with me. You and yo' bad decisions are the reason we're in this shit in the first place. You been doin' questionable shit since you met this girl. Hell, I'm gon' fuck around and have to put yo' grown ass on punishment. Swear y'all niggas gon' have me in the hospital in a minute. Killin' mutha-fuckas over pussy and tryna be super save a hoe. All y'all asses can get the fuck out my shit for real!" he grumbled, polishing off the last of his drink. When we weren't moving fast enough, he added,

"Meeting adjourned! Get moving!" He stood and made his way out of the room, presumably to meet our asses at the front door.

Zaakir was the first one out behind him with me following up closely, hoping to have a word with him outside. I ignored my OG calling my name and continued out. With this new shit going on with Zaakir, now definitely wasn't the time to hash out our issues. Just like I'd ignored her, though, Zaakir's ass ignored me and peeled out the driveway fast as hell, leaving my ass standing there looking stupid. I wasn't about to chase his crybaby ass down. I'd catch up with him later when he wasn't so deep in his feelings. For now, I was taking my ass home to my woman.

ZURI

Since Sevyn had flaked on me the other day, we were meeting up for lunch and a little shopping. I pulled into the mall parking lot and immediately spotted her primping in her car. My girl was so fine, and she seemed to be in a better headspace since that whole ridiculous case started. I really couldn't wait until Tramel got his, and I was hoping karma put a rush job on his comeuppance.

"Hey, boo!" she gushed, giving me a hug once I'd waddled over to her. "I missed you sooooo much! Don't be taking no more baecations without giving me at least a week's notice."

"Awww, I missed you too!" I giggled as we separated, and she waved a dismissive hand.

"Girl, I was talking to my nephew! Don't be kidnapping him no more. I almost put an Amber Alert out for him." She had the nerve to look serious, sending me into a fit of laughter.

"Get your crazy ass away from me."

"I mean, I missed you too." She shrugged.

"You get on my nerves."

"I love you too." I sucked my teeth, and she laughed as she looped her arm through mine. "Naw, but for real, though, how was the time away with your man? I see you all bronzed up and glowing!" she complimented, and I couldn't help smiling widely.

The time away had been perfect, and I felt like Shai and I were more connected than ever.

"It was great! Shai spent the whole time catering to me and making sure I was pampered! My ass was fall off the bone tender after all the massages and spa visits." I shuddered, just thinking about the way the masseuses had rubbed me down every day after our multiple excursions.

"Okaaaaay, I know that's right! Bro-in-law better make sure my girl good! I been saying my Ciara prayer every night 'cause I'm tired of the devil sending his minions in the form of a fine nigga. Hopefully, it works soon." She'd said it jokingly, but I sensed the sadness she was trying to mask in her tone and instantly slowed down.

She hadn't said too much about what she had going on with Zaakir since leaving his house, but obviously, she was going through it, and I felt bad as hell. There I was, bragging about my vacation when she was feeling some type of way about her relationship issues.

"Aww, Sev."

"Girl, do not start." She noticed my slowed pace and shrugged indifferently. "I'm good... really."

I couldn't help feeling bad about her situation despite what she said. Then again, I still held out hope for Zaakir. There had to be real feelings there after the way he'd acted when we all didn't know how things would turn out.

"I just... I don't like you going through this. You deserve so much more and—"

"I know yo' emotional ass ain't cryin', Zuri." She stopped completely, seeing my eyes misting, and I tried to sniffle back the tears threatening to fall. "Aww, boo, I promise I'm good, and even if I wasn't, I have bigger things to worry about than a man. I'm just happy you're getting your happily ever after. Now, suck up those tears so we can go tear this mall down." She wiped my tears away and locked hands with me, melting my heart. I knew right then that I would have to do something nice for her before the week was over.

"Okay, but I'm here if you need me. I don't care what I have going on. You can come to me about anything." I hoped she knew just how sincere I was.

A look I couldn't describe flashed across her face, but it was gone before I could identify it and replaced with a smile.

"I know, bestie. Now come on, so I can get my baby some more stuff to have him shittin' on these other babies." I decided to drop it and allowed her to pull me away.

After about a half hour, I'd put our conversation behind me and focused on the task at hand, which was filling up my baby's closet. By the time my stomach started growling, we'd been in just about every store that held baby items, and the smell of the food court had me shuffling in that direction. Sevyn instantly had her nose turned up at the idea, but I wasn't patient enough to drive through traffic to get to the Olive Garden where she wanted to go.

"Well, just let me grab a quick bite, and we can still go to Olive Garden 'cause now that you said something, I'm craving some chicken alfredo." I surrendered since she was still complaining as we stood in line at Panda Express.

"Greedy ass." She chuckled, shaking her head. "I'm tellin' Shai you out here feeding my nephew this bullshit as soon as I see him."

"Jokes on you 'cause Shai don't got no say so in what I eat. He gets me whatever I want." I stuck my tongue out as the line moved, and she laughed.

"Yeah, okay," she mumbled, and I took the opportunity to check my phone.

My cheeks hiked, seeing a text from Shai. He was always checking on me, especially since he'd been having to work more hours at the restaurant. Half the time, I was knocked out when he finally made it home, and when I woke up the next morning, he'd already be gone. We'd really been like two ships passing in the night, but he made sure to check on me throughout the day and order me lunch if I wasn't already out. I was understanding at the moment, but I really missed him and couldn't wait until he hired enough people so he could be home more.

"Uhhh, girl, do you know that bitch? 'Cause she staring hard as hell."

"Who?" I looked up, frowning, and scanned the area. There were only a few tables in the area we were in, so it wasn't hard to find Erica in the corner. I rolled my eyes at the sight of her staring me down like I'd stolen her husband. She really had a lot of nerve, especially when she had one of my bags on the table next to her. It was laughable, and I wasted no time putting my attention back on my phone. "That ain't nobody but Deshawn bum ass hoe, Erica."

Sevyn's eyes ballooned. "*That's* the bitch he left you for? It definitely makes sense, a bum for a bum." She shook her head, still staring a hole in her before narrowing her eyes. "And is that yo' Gucci bag his cheap ass bought you? Oh, hell naw!" Before I could stop her, she was already making her way across the room.

I followed her with a low groan. I wasn't trying to have any interactions with Deshawn's hoe, but I wasn't going to let Sevyn get into any more trouble.

"Awww, today's show is brought to you by the number ten," Erica said smartly as soon as we reached her table, causing Sevyn to suck her teeth and wave her off.

"A bitch wearing the next bitch's shit really shouldn't be running her mouth. You and yo' broke ass man couldn't afford to get you your own? It figures."

Laughing, Erica folded her hands on top of the table. "Well, it was the only thing I could actually fit that your frumpy ass friend left behind besides her man."

"Sevyn, she not even worth it, girl. Let's go." I tried to pull her away, but her crazy ass snatched out of my grip.

"Girl, you think wearing her hand me downs is a flex? You're really dumber than I thought." Sevyn smacked her lips. "Matter fact, give me this shit!" Huffing, she snatched the purse off the table. Before any of us could react, she turned it upside down and had Erica's stuff clamoring to the floor, drawing all eyes on us.

"Bitch, you got me fucked up!" Erica finally snapped out of the trance that had her stuck to her seat and jumped up, lunging at Sevyn, but Deshawn came out of nowhere and scooped her up.

We stood and watched as she struggled to get out of his grasp, but he kept a tight grip on her, turning her body away and making her kick their food off the table.

"Are you stupid? Stop before yo' ass ends up dead!" he hissed in her ear, but she only became more irate.

"Girl, let's go before I have to mace this muthafucka." Having had enough of the drama, Sevyn pulled me out the door and toward the mall exit.

"You still have the bag, though," I pointed out, and she looked down like she had already forgotten about it.

"Oh, I was just gon' throw this shit away. I just didn't want that bitch wearing it." Shrugging, she tossed it into the closest trash can and dramatically dusted her hands off.

"How you know I ain't want that?" I feigned shock, looking back.

"If you wanted it, you wouldn't have left that shit. Stop playin' with me. Shit probably wasn't even real anyway," she fussed. I damn near choked on my spit because I knew for a fact Deshawn's cheap ass hadn't gone into any Gucci store, and I'd only accepted it because, once upon a time, I loved him. It was laughable the things I'd put up with in the name of love, and I was so happy that I had a man who knew how to reciprocate everything I gave him. "I'll meet you at Olive Garden."

Sevyn snapped me out of my thoughts once we made it outside and reminded me that I was hungry. Her tough ass waited until I made it to my car and tossed everything in the trunk before climbing behind the wheel of her own. I'd barely dropped into my own seat before my phone dinged. My forehead bunched at the unknown number texting me. I opened it despite my unease of not knowing who the fuck it could've been and grew even more confused.

It was Deshawn checking to ensure that I wasn't going to tell Shai about what happened. I could sense his fear through the text and knew that whatever he'd done to my ex had to have been extensive to have Deshawn's shit talking ass so shook. I immediately cracked the fuck up as I pulled off, leaving him on read.

ZAAKIR

I waited for Shai's aggravating ass to hop in the car and sighed heavily when he finally did. Since that weak ass meeting at Casa's house, he'd been trying to be glued to my hip. He thought he was slick like I didn't know what he was doing, but the shit was as obvious as his ass being half-white. Ignoring the small talk he was trying to make, I smashed the gas, burning rubber as I pulled away.

"Damn, nigga, slow the fuck down!" he complained, mugging me as he rushed to put his seatbelt on.

I ignored him, picking up even more speed. Nobody told his ass to make me his chauffeur, but since he wanted to make me that, he was gon' have to deal with me being a speed demon. I turned the volume up on the Durk that was playing to drown his crying ass out and irritate him at the same time. It was already late as fuck, and he'd pulled me out of my bed to ride with him. He was lucky my bed was empty since Sevyn's ass was dodging me after the disappearing act I'd pulled. I was trying to give her time to cool off, but once I finished taking care of her issues, I was going to be right back over there.

I followed my GPS to the location he'd given me, and my eyes narrowed once we pulled up. I thought his ass had given me the wrong address when I saw Statesville prison in front of us. Cocking my head his way, my lip curled at the wide grin on his face.

"Nigga, what the fuck we doin' here?" I huffed, irritated and ready to knock his teeth down his throat if it meant he'd stop showing me those shits.

Opening his door, he paused and looked back at me. "You trust me?"

I absolutely trusted him, but the way he was moving had me questioning his ass. This whole shit was weird, but I still nodded to confirm that I did. His grin returned, and he motioned for me to follow him as he hopped out. I talked shit under my breath but followed him to the side of the building until we made it to a door with the words *Employee Entrance*. It was then that I noticed this nigga was cloaked in all black. Black hoodie, black jeans, black Air Force Ones. Before I could question him, he banged on the door twice, and it opened right up. A guard stuck his head out and looked us both up and down as he opened the door wider.

"Nigga, what the fuck you got me in this dirty ass mutha-fucka for?" I pressed lowly so the guard wouldn't hear me.

"Shhh, just chill. You gon' like this shit."

I didn't know what his ass had planned, but I figured it was some shit that one of our pops set up. It wasn't until we reached the cafeteria, and Sevyn's bitch ass husband came into view, that I understood. The last I'd heard, he wasn't even in a Chicago prison. I looked to my cousin for answers, not that any were needed for me to go upside that nigga's head.

"The dicks put his ass here, tryna keep him safe 'cause he supposed to be a witness against Sevyn." That had my neck snapping back like he'd just slapped the fuck out of me. I saw red as I rushed to open the door, but he stopped me. "I pulled some strings, but you gon' have to make the shit look like an accident. Preferably like he hung himself type shit." He turned and tapped the guard, who produced a face towel.

"Man, what the fuck?"

"Shit, you want his ass or not? I figured you'd wanna do the honors, but if you can't handle this shit, then I will, and you can just watch." He shrugged, pulling his jeans up on his waist, but I grabbed his shoulder before he could enter.

After all the shit Tramel had done, I wanted to take my time and make his bitch ass suffer. Knowing that I had limited time and options was a blow I wasn't expecting, but if anybody was going to kill that nigga, it was going to be me. Shai threw his hands up and backed away to give me room to go in.

Tramel had his back turned, looking as if he was trying to pump himself up for whatever was about to happen, but when he heard the door slam behind me, he whipped around. Confusion had his face frowned before recognition shined through, and he smirked.

"I was wondering who the fuck had enough pull to have me summoned." He sneered. "I should've known it had to be the great A'santi clan."

"Nigga, save that fuckin' small talk."

We raced toward each other, and he instantly tried to hit me with a right hook, but it barely glanced my chin. "Sevyn hit harder than that, bitch!"

The mention of Sevyn had him pulling out a shank and rushing me. I hadn't expected his ass to be holding if this whole shit was set up, but he was a slimy ass nigga, so it made sense. Shai had told me to make the shit clean, but him having a knife changed things. I sent a stiff uppercut to his stomach that had him doubling over, and on the way down, I cut his Adam's apple with my hand, sending him to his knees. It took everything in me not to beat his fucking head in, but I wasn't trying to have this shit come back on us or Sevyn, so I quickly wrapped each end of the towel around my hands and pulled it tightly around his neck. The shock had him dropping the knife, and he panicked even more. He immediately started thrashing around, but I kept my grip firm, steadying him with my own body.

Out of all the ways I'd killed people, this was the first time I'd choked somebody, and it would damn sure be the last. I wasn't expecting it to be so fucking tiring. It could've been due to how big that nigga Tramel was and how much of a fight he gave me. What should've only taken about five minutes felt like twenty, but once his body finally started to sag, I pulled tighter until he was completely still. Sweating and out of breath, I dropped his ass, and he hit the floor with a thud.

"Fuck!"

"Took yo' ass long enough!" Shai stuck his head in the door, gaining my attention. "Let's fuckin' go. We only got about fifteen minutes before headcount."

It took every bit of restraint I had not to kick or spit on that motherfucker as I walked away from him. Two corrections officers were already headed in to get him back to his cell and finish staging it. I met Shai back in the hallway, and no words needed to be spoken as he held his fist out, and I tapped it with my own.

The same guard from before led us back out the way we'd come, and we stopped only to slap a brick of cash in his hand. Despite not having killed that nigga the way I wanted to, I felt like a weight was lifted off my shoulders. I'd handled Sevyn's biggest opp, and now all I needed to do was get at his right hand and snatch the case against her right out of the police's hands.

A few nights later, I ignored a call from Britney's janky pussy ass as I pulled up to Sevyn's crib. I hadn't spoken to ol' girl since I'd found out my dick was clean, and I didn't have any intention of talking to her ass again. After a couple of seconds, she hit me with a text. It was a video of her playing in her pussy with drenched fingers. That shit had me stuck for a second, and my dick jumped involuntarily.

Boom! Boom! Boom!

My phone hit the floor, and I pulled my gun but lowered it when I saw Sevyn's face looming in my window. I quickly rolled it down, unbothered by the look on her face or the fact that she was banging on my window like she was trying to break my shit. "Leave, Zaakir! I don't want yo' flaky ass over here!" She was screaming and going off in her dead silent neighborhood, but I was completely taken by how beautiful she looked.

Clad in only a robe and some long ass UGG boots with her hair up in a loose ponytail, she had me wanting nothing more than to carry her fine ass up to her bed. Licking my lips, I cut the engine and picked my phone up. I stuffed it down in my pocket as I eyed her from head to toe and climbed out of my car, walking up on her since she'd taken a couple of steps back.

"Stop fuckin' screamin' and actin' all crazy, man."

"Fuck you! Stay yo' ass away from me!"

"You don't mean that shit. Bring yo' goofy ass in the house so you can ride my face before I go to sleep."

"I don't—" She stopped abruptly as my words sank in, and I nodded, flashing my teeth at her salaciously. "No! I don't want shit from you, not even no damn head!"

"You sure?" I teased before holding up my hands as I continued to close the space between us. "Ayite, come on, I ain't tryna do this shit with you, bae. I'm tired as hell, and I ain't tryna wait on you to fall asleep so I can let myself in. Just let me in there now, and I'll stroke that lil' pussy 'til you get tired." I hated to sound like I was begging, but either my tone or my words had the fight leaving her just enough for me to wrap my arms around her.

The added effects of soft kisses on her neck had her body melting into mine, and I lifted her off her feet with a hand under each thigh. My dick was already straining against my sweats, feeling the heat emanating from her center, even in the brisk weather.

"Where have you been, Zaakir? I woke up, and you were just gone. No call, no text, nothing." Her voice was muffled as I carried her inside, locking the door behind us. I didn't respond, only continued to kiss her soft neck, allowing my tongue to explore the area. That only shut her up for a few seconds. "Zaakir."

She shuddered, and I took that as the green light to keep going. We made it to the stairs, and I slipped my hand under her robe, cursing when I felt how wet she was. "Fuuuuck, baby, all this for me?" I asked, biting into her neck and applying pressure to her swollen nub. Her back arched as I ascended the stairs and carried her into her bedroom. I sat on the edge of her bed so she was on top of me and lay back. "Come put that pussy on my tongue, Sev."

I wanted to taste her right then; I ain't even care about taking my shit off. She had her face buried in her hands, and I realized the reason she hadn't done what I'd said was because she was crying. I rubbed her thighs, unsure of what to say, before I decided to lift her until her knees were planted by my ears.

"Zaa-kir." My name came out broken when I swiped my tongue through her slit. The tears never stopped flowing as I assaulted her pearl, and she quivered, biting her lip.

"Look at me." I paused long enough to order before latching onto her again, but she only squeezed her eyes closed tighter. I felt her trying to lift off me, and I locked her in place, moving my tongue rapidly.

"Mmmh!"

"Open yo' eyes and watch me make this pussy cum!" My voice was more forceful, and with one arm wrapped around her thigh, I reached up and pinched her nipple hard enough to make her lids flutter open. By then, she was winding her hips, unable to refuse me now that she was on the edge of an orgasm. Lust filled her face, but there wasn't shit but heated rage shining in her eyes as she looked down at me.

"Ohh shit, shit, shit! I-I'm cummin'!" Her movements became faster and more rigid, and she could no longer stop her eyes from rolling as she came, flooding my face with her nectar. She was still whimpering and breathing heavily as her body fell to the side.

I took the opportunity to slip out of bed, pulling my shirt and hoodie off together. I then freed myself from my sweats. She was now on her side, and I pushed her robe away, licking my way up her body, but she was no longer under her orgasmic spell.

"Don't touch me!" She huffed, shooting daggers at me as she flopped onto her back and tried to weakly fight me to pull her robe back down. Once again, her eyes were glistening, and I fell on top of her. "Get off me, you fucking liar! You don't love me! You can't love me and treat me like this!"

I can't lie; I was taken aback by how emotional she was and the shit she was saying. True, I had dipped after the last time I'd seen her, but it was to get my thoughts together and try to handle some of the shit she had going on. I forced her face my way, giving it a light squeeze until she stopped trying to snatch away.

"Sev! Sev, look at me!" I demanded until she brought her glare from above my head to meet my eyes. Like any other woman, she needed more than just me showing and doing to prove my love. She needed me to affirm that shit for her, and while I thought I'd done that, it clearly wasn't enough. "I don't know what else I can do to show you that I love yo' crazy ass! I'm out here growing a liver, killing muthafuckas, and all types of shit, and you *still* tryna question me. What the fuck you want? Like, fuck you want me to do, slit my wrist and bleed?"

All my confession did was make her cry harder, like the ugly kind that had her face unrecognizable. I tried my hardest to kiss all her tears away, telling her over and over again that I loved her. I'd never in my life gave a fuck about how my actions made a woman feel, but in that moment, I knew I couldn't stomach seeing her crying because of me. I rolled off her, pulled her body closer to mine, and held her until she fell asleep.

SEVYN

As stupid as it sounds, I was still surprised to wake up to an empty bed after Zaakir had put me to sleep with a lullaby of I love yous. I really needed to get my level of delusion under control. When I saw his ass pull up, I was ready for a drag out, knock down fight, where I would've been able to get my feelings off my chest. I thought I'd finally feel *better*, feel *vindicated*, but he barely had to breathe on me, and my legs had spread like butter in addition to my emotional floodgates opening. Then he put his tongue on me, and I lost my fucking mind!

The fact that even after all that and him leaving me in the middle of the night, I was still disappointed was just another testament to how delusional I was. Tossing my covers back, I swung my legs over the side of the bed just as somebody started pounding on my front door despite me having a fucking doorbell. I searched for my phone so I could see who it was and sighed when I realized it was downstairs. I considered leaving whoever was out there knocking until they eventually left so I could wallow in my misery. That thought was quickly dismissed, though, after five minutes had passed, and they were still out there.

Groaning, I finally made my way downstairs, dragging my feet the whole way, but I immediately tightened up when I locked eyes with Detective Hill through the glass. It was way too damn early to deal with him, and if he hadn't seen me, I would've snuck my ass back upstairs. I opened the door with clenched teeth, and he pushed his way inside.

"Mrs. Ellis," he growled, advancing on me. "I'm here to inform you that your husband hung himself a few days ago," he said, and I narrowed my eyes at him suspiciously.

The police lied so much. There was no telling if his ass was just saying that to scare me for whatever reason. I had to admit his poker face was good as fuck, but the fact that I didn't see any deception and only anger told me everything I needed to know. Gasping, I turned away, feeling like I was about to have a panic attack.

"Sssso, what does this mean? What about the case?" My breathing picked up, and I fell onto the bench nearby.

The deal had been to try and get his plug so I could get off, but without Tramel, I wasn't sure there'd still be a deal. He talked a good game, but he didn't trust anybody, and I knew he'd kept his plug a secret even from Rome.

"That's not the type of question a wife should be asking when she just found out her husband is dead." His tone had my gaze shooting to him, and I could see the accusation there.

Sucking my teeth, I stood, wishing I could slap his paranoid ass.

"What the fuck else should I be askin'? That nigga tried to kill me. He actually did kill my baby, and then he set me up, which is why I'm even having to work with yo' ass in the first place. Excuse my French, but fuck Tramel Ellis! For all I care, his ass can go straight to hell! All I'm worried about is getting me and my staff out of this mess he put us In!" It seemed like he was trying to look through me and gauge if I was telling the truth or not. After a few seconds, I guess he decided that I was.

"I don't know what's going to happen with your deal," he admitted, raking a hand through his greasy hair. "My superiors are scrambling because they still want the connect, but Rome is still missing, and honestly, all of this shit just looks... almost too convenient." His tone still held a level of suspicion, and I shook my head in disbelief.

"Don't look at me! I don't benefit at all from anything happening to my husband or his little lap dog." He was really starting to get on my nerves, and if it wasn't for the possibility that I could end up working with someone much worse, I'd report his ass, and that was only *if* they were willing to give me a different detective to work with.

"Regardless, you're a flight risk, and they'll probably want me to place you in custody to ensure that you don't run—"

"Oh, hell naw, let me call my lawyer 'cause you're crazy as hell if you think I'ma let you lock me up just because that nigga killed hisself!" I was already on my feet to get my phone with him right on my heels, talking shit like a true cop.

"You must've forgot," he taunted. "Your lawyer is dead, and even if he wasn't, there's no guarantee that it's anything he could've done for you, considering the agreement you signed." That quickly froze me in my spot just as I went to dial Brian. I'd forgotten all about him randomly being killed, and now when shit was getting really hectic, I didn't have a backup in place.

"Well, this just happened, so you have to give me a chance to get legal representation," I said, hoping I sounded much more confident than I felt.

"Slow your roll. Locking you up would just be precautionary, but I haven't even talked to anyone to find out if that's necessary. Just... just stay by your phone and don't leave the city." He hit me with a warning look before spinning on his heels. "I'll let myself out." I watched him walk away, and it wasn't until I heard the door close behind him that I released a breath I didn't know I was holding.

I was still sitting in the same spot almost twenty minutes later when my door opened again, and I hurried to make sure it wasn't Hill's annoying ass again. I'd had time to think, and this time, if he said anything I didn't like, I was going to curse him out. Imagine my surprise when Zaakir was the person standing there with bags of food and a tray of drinks.

"Damn, I tried to make it back before you woke up." I hated how cute he looked when he wasn't sure of himself and how it immediately made me put my guard down. "You hungry?" he asked, and as if my stomach was trying to answer for me, it growled loudly, and he grinned triumphantly.

"I guess I can eat." Without waiting for him, I headed back to the kitchen and pulled down a couple of plates for us.

"I just grabbed a bunch of shit. I didn't know what you—"

"Tramel's dead," I blurted, cutting him off as I set our plates down on the island in front of him. "He hung himself, I guess. Now, the detective is saying he doesn't know what's gonna happen with the case, so they might try to put me back in jail since I'm apparently a flight risk and don't have a lawyer."

Despite the bomb I'd just dropped on him, the most reaction I got was a raised brow as he continued pulling out the many containers of food he had. It really shouldn't have alarmed me because Zaakir was usually calm, cool, and collected with a joke for every occasion, but the problem was, his ass didn't seem surprised at all.

In fact, he was talking like he hadn't heard shit I'd said. "This pancakes right here, and this French toast." He stacked the containers on top of each other and went to pull out more.

"Did you just hear me? Tramel's dead, and I might be going to jail!" Casually, he continued to lay the food out with a shrug.

"You ain't goin' to jail," was his simple response, and my brows instantly dipped.

A week ago, his ass was just finding out about my involvement with the police, and now, all of a sudden, he had insider information to know that I wasn't going to get locked up. It wasn't lost on me that he'd completely glazed over Tramel being dead, and it made sense to an extent because he hated that nigga and wanted to kill him after what he'd done. Was it possible that he could've had something to do with him dying? I eyed him as he started shoveling food onto his plate.

My stomach rumbled again, reminding me that I was actually hungry, and I reached for the pancakes. "How do you know?"

I wasn't trying to sound doubtful, but if he was privy to some vital information, I needed to know ASAP. He sighed, finally done dressing up his plate with a mountain of food, and looked at me with his fork poised in the air.

"I know 'cause Campbell's been handling your case since Brian's... accident, and he already talked to those pathetic ass detectives. Hill wasn't supposed to come over here and say shit, and definitely nothing about locking you back up."

His answer only confused me more, and I wondered when he'd had time to set all that up in the last couple of weeks. But before I could open my mouth, he shushed me with a finger. "You don't need to know shit else but that everything is handled already. Now, can I please finish my damn food in peace? At least if you gon' be interrupting my meal, you could be askin' about some important shit, like if I really meant what I said last night or whatever else y'all women be stressing y'all self out about." He grunted around a mouthful of French toast.

I knew I was supposed to be worried about a possible prison sentence, but my heart was exploding in my chest at that moment. For some reason, I trusted him, and more importantly, I trusted what he was saying. I immediately clocked my delusion rearing its ugly head, but that didn't stop me from doing what he'd told me.

"Okay, so *did* you mean any of the shit you said last night?" I couldn't keep the sarcasm out of my tone.

"Every muthafuckin' word," he said, flashing his teeth cockily. "We do need to talk about why yo' ass ain't said it back yet. You're like fifty and O right now, baby. Usually, when a muthafucka says I love you, the woman says..."

"I love you too, Zaakir."

SHAI

Meeting with my parents had been a long time coming, and today, I was going to handle that. I'd planned to talk to them separately since I had different issues to address with them both, but when I pulled up to Queen's crib, his car was out front. I passed his men with a chuckle and knocked on the door, opting not to use my key, so I didn't walk in on some shit that would leave me blind.

It took some time for her to answer, and when she did, her eyes ballooned in surprise. "Shai, baby, why didn't you use your key?" She ushered me in, unable to keep the smile off her face. If I wasn't sure of shit else, I was sure that my OG loved the fuck out of me, and it was evident all over her face.

"I saw Gio's car out there." I shrugged, leaving it at that as I returned the quick hug she gave me.

Her brows dipped before understanding shined through, and she giggled girlishly, scratching the back of her neck.

"Ohhh, okay, well, come on in. Your—Giorgio's in the living room." She shooed me on while she locked the door behind us.

I traveled through the house until I made it to her dining room, where Gio was sitting on the sofa with one leg folded over the other. When he saw me enter, he hurried to his feet and stuck his hand out, just as happy to see me, if not more so.

"How're you, son?" I silently shook his hand, giving him a stiff nod in response. That shit didn't seem to deter him at all, probably because I didn't immediately correct him for calling me son, and he stepped back with a sweeping gesture. "Have a seat."

"You want something to drink or anything, baby?" Queen entered, sounding like Suzie Homemaker, but I instantly declined.

"Nah, I'm straight. I wasn't planning to stay long. Zuri was back at the house packing, and if I let her, she'll be tryna move that shit too." I smiled, thinking about her stubborn ass. It had been hard to get her to take it easy because she still thought she could do everything, and I was sure if they hadn't taken her off of work, she'd still be going in there, too.

"Okay, well, what brings you by?" she asked and dropped into the seat next to Gio.

I couldn't help noticing how comfortable they looked and knew this wasn't some new shit. The last thing I was trying to think about was them being on some creep shit, but I wondered how long they'd been fooling around behind my back despite her telling me I could kill his ass not too long ago. I went to speak, but Giorgio cut me off.

"Look, Shai, I just want you to know that my intentions behind what happened were never to hurt you. It's just something we all must do. I don't think any of us considered the political climate or the tension between blacks—" He caught himself, eyes sliding my mama's way before he quickly tried to correct it. "I mean African Americans and the police. I just want you to know I still would like you to resume your position if that's what you want to do. Also, as much as it would disappoint me, I'd be okay with you declining the position, but it's whatever you want."

I took my time answering and stroked my beard as I considered. I hadn't given it much thought because since we'd come back from Jamaica, I'd been swamped, but I did still want to take my place at the head. Like my mama said, it was mine, and more than that, I deserved it.

"Honestly, I was considering not taking it after that whole thing, but despite how fucked up it was, it doesn't make sense to give up after all the hard work and time I put in. Going forward, though, I'm gon' need you to be honest about every aspect of this process, down to the smallest detail, or I'm gonna walk away for good." It seemed like he didn't even hear the threat because he was grinning so widely.

"Good, good. We can resume business as soon as possible. I already got a couple of things lined up for you."

"Actually, hold off on that until after we get this shit figured out with Sevyn. I don't know if her connection to us will have them looking our way since Tramel's dead. Just give me a couple of weeks." I spoke methodically, and if it were possible, Gio's grin got bigger, and he nodded proudly, just like my mama.

"Spoken like a true Don."

I waited a few seconds before moving on to the next issue I wanted to address. "Now that that's out the way. Y'all wanna finally tell me when y'all started back messing around?" I asked, making the smile slip from both their faces. They immediately began to fidget uncomfortably, looking like two children who were caught with their hands in the cookie jar.

"Son—" Giorgio went to speak first, but Queen cut him off with a tap on his arm.

"I don't know what you think you know, Shai, but you're really way off mark and outta pocket." The tone and choice of words she used had me laughing, and she glared at me.

"I'm outta pocket? Queen, you hated this muthafucka for as long as I can remember, and now he's grooming me to take over, and y'all's asses together every time I see y'all—"

"We're your parents, so we should have a cordial relationship." She shrugged weakly.

"I'ma grown ass man, bro. It ain't like y'all co-parenting. To be real, it really ain't my business, but—actually, it is my business because if y'all's little relationship don't work out, it's gon' put me in a fucked up position." She drew back like I'd slapped her and then cocked her head at me, dropping her nice act.

"First of all, watch yo' damn mouth. You ain't that much of a grown ass man! Secondly, I'm the real grown muthafucka around here, me and your father, and if I wanna fuck on my baby daddy, then that's what I'm gon' do! Yo' ass got a whole baby mama at home but over here in our business. I know you better get the fuck on!" She was going off.

Giorgio tried to place a comforting hand on her thigh, but she'd clearly gone off the deep end. I personally didn't care. Was it weird that she was fucking with him like that? Yes. I'd spent my whole life hating this nigga on our behalf, but as an adult, it really had no bearing over my life. I just wanted her ass to admit it and stop trying to sneak around.

Laughing, I threw my hands up in surrender. "You got it, Queen. If you wanna get back with yo' white baby daddy, that's cool. But if you're so grown, why you was hiding it?"

"I wasn't ready to admit it to myself or anybody else that I still have feelings for his ass, especially after I talked so much shit and was going around wishing death on him and shit. Sorry, bae, but you really was on some good bullshit." She quickly apologized before continuing. "I guess we can come out of hiding, though. If our son is over here lecturing us, that's bad."

"You talkin' 'bout me, shit, everybody already on to y'all asses. You ain't low." She seemed shocked by the news, eyes bucking as she clutched her chest.

"Really? You think so?"

"Amore, you're the only one who thinks no one knows," Gio gently said, even as he fought not to laugh and failed once I let mine slip, making her snatch her hand out of his with narrowed eyes.

"Fuck y'all!" She huffed, jumping to her feet and storming off toward the kitchen.

Gio's chuckling instantly turned into a cough fit out of fear that he'd be in the doghouse. He went to chase after her but thought better of it and dropped back into his seat with a shrug.

Deciding to give him an out, I stood. "I'ma head on home," I said, immediately thinking of the infamous SpongeBob meme as he stood as well.

"Okay, well, you don't only have to talk to me when it comes to business, son. We'd really love for you and Zuri to stop by for dinner. This time, without the boxing match."

"I'll see what I can do," I told him, moving toward the door.

I wasn't opposed to having dinner with my parents, but only after Zuri had the baby and wasn't at risk because the way our families were set up, there was no telling what would kick off.

When I finally left, I went straight home to help Zuri with packing. Since we were doing it, the shit took much longer than it would've if we had just hired a moving company like I'd wanted to. When I brought that shit up to her, she'd immediately rejected it, talking about not liking the idea of other people touching her stuff. As ridiculous as her paranoia was, I was willing to do whatever she wanted if it made her happy, and since she'd picked out our forever home, she'd been happy as hell packing everything, albeit slowly. I, on the other hand, had used a moving company, so all my shit was packed up and over at the new house already.

When I got to her crib, I found her packing up her bathroom, but when she saw the Panera bread bag in my hand, she instantly stopped. "Oooh, is that for me?" Her face lit up as I helped her out of the office chair she was sitting in and gave her a couple quick kisses.

"Of course, love." My lips curved up, seeing her do her happy dance once she was on her feet. "Yo' ass too funny," I told her, shaking my head.

"Well, you're the one who keeps bringing me food. I'm convinced you're tryna have me on my 600-lb Life," she joked, taking the bag from me as she waddled out of the bathroom, and just like a lost puppy, I followed right behind her with my hands on her waist.

"Mmmhmm, and I'ma be right on there with you, washing between yo' rolls and bringing you obscene amounts of food."

Her head fell back as she fell into a fit of laughter, and I used the opportunity to plant kisses on her neck.

"You're a mess. Get off me." She tried to bump me away, feigning an attitude, but I held on tight.

"Naw, I'm dead ass. I'ma be greasing yo' ass up so you can fit in the car when we go see Dr. Now and everything."

"Oooh, you make me sick! Move!"

"Quit pushin' yo' ass on me like that, 'fore I have you bent over, love. I know you don't want yo' food getting cold," I threatened, loosening my grip on her waist just enough for her greedy ass to scamper away squealing.

Beaming, she plopped down on the edge of the bed and started digging her food out.

"I'll finish the bathroom while you eat." I slipped out of my Nike Tek jacket and tossed it on a nearby chair, but she stopped me with bucked eyes.

"No! I don't want you mixing my stuff up. You can do the... closet. Yeah, do the closet." She waved me away before stuffing some bread in her mouth.

"Ayite, *boss.*"

The closet was better for me anyway since I'd be able to get more packed in there. I grabbed one of the boxes she had stacked up in the corner and ducked inside her walk-in closet. I was thankful Zuri was the type of woman who felt like everything had a place and made sure she put stuff where it belonged. It took no time to pack up her clothes, then I started on her shoes. By the time I got to her accessories and shit, she was knocked out and snoring with one hand on her belly. I didn't want to wake her, but I couldn't resist pecking her soft, pouty lips and kissing my son, who began to kick the spot I was in. Zuri didn't even flinch as if she couldn't feel it, but I could literally see him pushing against her skin. Shit was crazy, and I watched in amazement until my phone rang, and I rushed out, closing the door behind me so I didn't disturb Zuri.

Seeing Carla's name on my screen had me sighing and hesitating to answer. She hadn't really been on shit since the last time, but her ass was beginning to make me uneasy, and I was on the verge of firing her. I took so long answering that it went to voicemail, and she called right back, letting me know it was something serious.

"Hello?"

"Oh, my God, Shai! There's been an accident at Suave! You need to get here now!

Shit! Just when I thought I was gon' have a good day!

ZAAKIR

"Daaaaaamnn!" My eyes widened at the damage to Shai's restaurant.

When that nigga messaged me, I never expected that he was talking about an actual accident. There was a whole ass car in the window of his shit. The whole block was full of nosey ass people and police cars, so I had to park up the street and walk back down. I could hear different people talking about what they saw or what they'd heard as I passed them, and from the sound of it, some random ass drunk driver had floored it and lost control of their vehicle. That shit sounded crazy as hell to me, and once I made it in front of the actual restaurant, I knew exactly why. It was Kendra's fucking BMW sticking out the window, and I covered my mouth with a closed fist.

"This is a crime scene. You need to step back, sir!" a random police officer came out of nowhere, trying to back me away without touching me.

"Man, this my cousin shit. Get the fuck on!" I scoffed and pushed right past him, only to be met by three more.

"Sir!"

"Aye, let him through. He's good!" Shai came out right in time because I was getting fed up with the cordial approach. They all looked disgruntled as they moved aside but knew better than to say shit.

"Nigga, tell me that ain't Kendra shit?" I quizzed in disbelief, even though I was seeing the shit with my own eyes. He shot me a look as we stepped over glass, confirming what I already knew, and I shook my head. "That bitch for real crazy. Where she at? She survived this shit?" The car was totally wrecked, and I knew if she was alive, her legs were crushed to pieces.

"The ambulance just left with her a lil' bit ago. They said she was alive when they pulled her out, but they didn't know if she was going to make it. Actually, I need to head up there. I'm just waiting on these muthafuckas to leave." My forehead bunched, but before I could ask, he explained. "It ain't even like that. I just want to make sure her crazy ass is okay, but I'm definitely pressing charges."

"Oh, shit, 'cause I thought you was bouta go tell their asses to pull the plug on that hoe," I cracked, gaining an irritated look from him as a detective approached with a pen and pad.

My natural reaction to one of them being that close to me was to tense up, especially after getting arrested not too long ago. It always felt like they were looking for something to put on somebody, whether the shit made sense or not, and that had me uneasy as fuck in the presence of one.

"Mr. A'santi, I have a few more questions before we head out." He adjusted his stance, looking between his paper and Shai.

"I already told y'all everything I know. I wasn't even an eyewitness. My manager called me up here." I could tell his patience with them was wearing thin, but the detective's own spidey senses must have been broken because he kept pushing.

"Right, right. Your manager said this woman is your ex. Can you tell me the last time you spoke with her?"

Shai's eyes narrowed on the man who was about a foot shorter, and he shoved his hands in his pockets, likely to prevent himself from knocking dude's ass out. "I already told that other detective that's walkin' around this muthafucka. I ain't talked to

Kendra's crazy ass in weeks. We've been broken up, and I don't know what the fuck she did this goofy ass shit for."

The detective scribbled as Shai spoke, pausing at the broken up part just briefly, and I blew out an exaggerated breath. He was already trying to piece shit together, and I let out a low groan.

"Here the fuck we go."

"Was the reason for this break up her sister Zuri, who you're having a baby with?"

"Man, if you don't get the fuck on!" Shai advanced, sending the man stumbling backward before he addressed the array of officers nearby. "Aye, one of y'all muthafuckas get y'all brethren the fuck away from me before y'all asses really have a reason to charge me!"

The detective gave one of those tight-lipped smiles that white people loved to do and backed away with his hands up before Shai could make good on his threat. He was trying to look tough, but his ass damn near grew wings and flew out of the area.

"Man, fuck this. I'm up," Shai grumbled, turning on his heels.

I fell into step beside him. "I'm riding with you. I ain't tryna miss the show."

I wasn't surprised that my crazy ass cousin actually went to the hospital to check on Kendra's nut ass, but I was surprised that her mama wasn't up there blocking and being in her daughter's business as usual. I was low key salty that I wasn't gonna get to see her show her natural ass. She'd been getting off easy, but I knew if she pushed Shai far enough, he'd have Aunty pull up and have her ass sharing a hospital room with her daughter. The thought had me laughing internally, and I silently hoped she'd pop up on some messy shit while we were still there.

Fuck!

I'd been hanging around Sevyn and occasionally listening while she watched ratchet TV, and the shit was rubbing off. Not only was I ready to instigate some shit, but I was using words like *messy*. I made a mental note to unsubscribe me and her ass from anything that shit was playing on.

Since Kendra was still in surgery, we had to sit out in the waiting room. It was crowded as fuck, and I hurried to snatch up the only chairs left in the room, which, thankfully, weren't too close to anyone. Shai's ass immediately got on his phone while I tuned into an episode of *The Simpsons* on the TV.

By the time the episode went off, though, I was ready to go. That was until a commotion at the nurse's station had me perking up. As expected, Kendra's ratchet ass mama had arrived and was putting on a show. Cheesing, I sat up in my chair, waiting for her to notice Shai, but she caught sight of her baby daddy first.

They instantly started arguing, and the nurse had to tell them to calm down or get out, which only had her turning up more as she made her way over to the waiting room. "This bitch," Shai grumbled, slinking down to try and hide like a pussy, but that didn't stop her from seeing his pale ass.

"What are *you* doing here?" Her nose turned up as she stopped short at the entrance, causing her baby daddy to run into her back. Every head in the room turned to Shai, mine included. "You probably did this, trying to get rid of her so you could be with that jezebel you cheated with!"

"Gone 'head, April. I ain't on that shit with you." He pinched the bridge of his nose with a sigh.

"Well, leave then! You don't have no business here anyway, demon!"

"Look, Shai, I really think you should just go." Zuri's dad tried to reason like his ass wasn't half to blame for his crazy ass daughter.

"Man, don't talk to me. I ain't forgot the weird shit yo' ass did at that dinner. I ain't goin' nowhere. I'ma stay right here, and y'all can take y'all's asses over there somewhere."

"You don't tell me what to do. I'm here for *my* daughter! Yo' ass need to go before I have security come and make you go!" she shouted, and when he didn't attempt to leave, she only grew more irate. "Security! Security!"

"You just gon' let her talk to you crazy and snitch on you too?" I instigated.

"Man, shut the fuck up!" Shai shot me a warning look, and I shrugged, pulling my phone from my pocket.

"Don't get mad at me, nigga. She the one cussin' yo' ass out." He shook his head and stood as the security guards finally came to intervene. They started talking over each other, explaining their side of the story, but April's was a much louder version.

I was able to make out what the security guard told her and immediately grew bored. "Ma'am, we can't kick anyone out of the emergency room. Go have a seat, and once you get to the back, then you can take up your issues with one of the nurses."

"Oh, this some bullshit! How is anybody supposed to be safe if y'all just letting threatening ass people in here?" Spittle flew from her mouth, and I could tell they were getting just as irritated with her as everybody else.

"Look, you're the only one in here causing a disturbance, and if you don't stop, you'll be the one they have escorted out of here. Now, lower your voice and find somewhere to sit!"

She waved them off nastily and dropped into the closest chair she could find with her puppy dog behind her. It was hardly quiet for a full minute when Miss Zora and Zuri walked in looking confused, and I pulled up the camera on my phone.

"Kadeem, what—"

"OH, HELL NAW!" April was right back on her feet, and Ms. Zora moved to stand in front of her as Shai raced over. "WHAT THE FUCK IS THIS BITCH DOIN HERE!"

"Oh, I got yo' bitch! Kadeem, you better get yo' baby mama!"

"Look, all of y'all need to calm down!" Kadeem jumped between them and then turned to April's crazy ass. "I called them up here because Zuri needs to be here for her sister in her time of need. They're sisters, and she has the right to be here just like you and me." He lamely tried to reason, setting both women off again.

Shai had already moved Zuri to the side and was talking to her lowly, but whatever he was saying got interrupted by Ms. Zora and April shouting.

"I should've known this was some bullshit. I can promise you, this will be the last time you ever play in me and my daughter's face!" Ms. Zora was about to walk away, but April's ass had to get the last word.

"Girl, fuck you and yo' daughter!" she shouted.

Ms. Zora did a ninja move, spinning around and hitting the woman with boxer precision. I was glad I'd pulled my phone out because she was whooping April's ass. Shai left a distraught looking Zuri to run over and try to help Kadeem separate the women. Security entered the melee, and they were finally able to pull them apart, but Ms. Zora had a firm grip on April's hair and wasn't letting go.

It took them a minute to detach her hand from April's head, and all eyes were on them as they argued back and forth with security. However, my eyes were on Zuri, who looked more than just upset. Her face was pinched in discomfort, and she was holding her stomach. Since her baby daddy was preoccupied, I got up to see what was wrong when she started peeing on herself.

"Yoooo, what the fuck, Zuri? Not you peeing on yourself, girl. You lucky I ain't get that on camera."

"This ain't pee, fool. My water just broke!"

ZURI

P ain tore through my midsection, and I squeezed my eyes shut. It couldn't be happening again. There was no way I was losing my baby after making it so far. I clutched my stomach and started making my way over to Shai since his ass still hadn't noticed what was going on.

"Hold up, Z. Sit down until I can get a nurse over here." Zaakir's ignorant ass grabbed my arm, stopping me. I started to slap his hand away, but another piercing pain had me dropping into the seat. "Aye, man, something wrong with Zuri!" Zaakir shouted, and all eyes shot my way.

Shai rushed over with Kadeem's ass following closely, and they both wore worried expressions.

"I-I think my water just broke," I panted, squeezing my eyes closed again. I didn't want to see the look of disappointment or pity on anybody's face when I was already feeling so bad, and I damn sure wasn't trying to look at Shai.

"Look at her sick ass, tryna take the attention off my baby—" April's voice rang out over the crowd, and I rolled my eyes.

"Can y'all please do your job and get this bitch out of here?" my mama snapped at the guards, and they hurriedly pulled them both away, fighting as a nurse made it to me.

"Ma'am, I need to help you get into the wheelchair. Do you think you can stand?"

"I got it." Shai wasted no time lifting me into the wheelchair, and all I could do was repeat how sorry I was.

I knew better than to listen to my dad. He'd been one of the biggest stressors my entire pregnancy, but when my mama called and told me that we needed to get to the hospital, I thought the worst. He'd worded it in a way to make it seem like he was hurt or being admitted, and we both fell for that shit without asking any questions. I couldn't really blame him solely for what was happening since his ex was up there clowning, but I would've never been there to witness it if it wasn't for him.

"Fuck you apologizing for, love? Just calm down so they can see what's going on." Shai pressed a kiss to my head before the nurse wheeled me off. He gripped my hand in his and walked beside us.

"Sir, you're gonna have to stay—"

"I'm the father, so I'm going wherever they go," he said with finality, shutting her right up.

Shai stayed by my side even when they got me to the room and a doctor came in to examine me. Another nurse hooked me up to different machines while the doctor, who wasn't my usual physician, checked my cervix.

"This baby is coming tonight. I need you all to get the room prepped."

My eyes widened, and I shot a nervous look at Shai. "What! It's too early! Can't you, like, stop it!" I was full of panic as I watched the nurses rushing in and out of the room, moving stuff around and bringing shit in.

"Zuri, I know this is scary, but you need to try to calm down. Your stress is the baby's stress, and we don't want your blood pressure spiking. There's really nothing else we can do besides deliver when the water sac has already burst, but I promise we're gonna take good care of you." The news that they were going to take out my baby had my eyes rolling, and everything went black.

. . .

The monotonous beeping of a machine roused me awake, and I was surprised to see the sun shining into my room. I gasped as it all came back to me, and my hands fell to my stomach, scaring me even more by how flat and sore it was. How the hell I was able to deliver a baby while unconscious? I'd never know, but apparently, it had been done.

Before I could speak, Shai was at my bedside, looking down at me with a grim expression that instantly stopped my heart. "Baby, you're up." He lifted my hand from my belly and kissed the back of it, which did nothing to comfort me.

"Where's our baby?" I swallowed hard, staring down at our locked hands to avoid seeing his face.

"Uh—" His hesitation had hot tears sliding down my face, and my chest caved. "Don't cry, love. They had to give you a c-section because the baby was in distress. He's in the NICU right now. They said with the type of complications he has, they don't know if he's going to make it or not, but he's strong. I know he's gonna pull through."

Any relief I might have felt quickly disappeared with the news that my baby was possibly going to die. I didn't even know what was worse, him dying in the womb or after he'd taken his first breath, and my heart ached for him.

"Can I go see him? Take me to him!" I pleaded, tears blurring my vision.

"Calm down, love—"

"Stop saying that shit! Just take me to my son!" I winced, feeling like I was being torn in half. My hand shot to my stomach as the machines started going off.

"You gotta see the doctor first, but you need to chill the fuck out! Your blood pressure is high as fuck right now!" he snapped, pressing the call button, but a nurse was already walking through the door.

She ran over to check the machines, and once she got them

quiet, she turned to me with a sympathetic expression. "Good morning, honey. I'm Tisha, your nurse for the next few hours. I know you're probably taking in a lot right now, but you have to keep your blood pressure down and try not to move too suddenly, or you might tear your stitches. Now, is it alright if I check on your incision?"

"Will I be able to see my baby after?" I quizzed eagerly. I didn't give a damn about the stitches or anything else; I just wanted to lay eyes on my son. She looked uneasy like she didn't want to answer and piss me off, and I can't say I blamed her. I had full intentions of tearing this shit up if they didn't give me access to my son.

"The doctor will need to clear you first. I'll check you out, then go get him so we can get you upstairs to see your little angel, okay? It'll take maybe five minutes tops if everything looks good." She waited for me to give her the go-ahead, and after a few seconds, I nodded, even though I thought this whole thing was stupid. I was really surprised by how fast it actually went. Like she said, she had checked my incision and vitals and left to retrieve the doctor in minutes.

When the door swung back open, my eyes filled with tears at the sight of my mama. Seeing that I was awake, she rushed over and gave me a gentle hug. "Aww, my poor baby! It's gonna be okay, Zeebee, don't cry!" She sounded like she was on the verge of crying herself as she rubbed my back and spoke softly. "I just came back from seeing him, and he's gorgeous. You did so good, and I'm so proud of you." After a minute, she held me at arm's length and wiped my face as the doctor entered. My mama gripped one of my hands while Shai held the other, listening intently.

His mouth was moving, but I honestly didn't even catch his name because I was too busy nodding and agreeing. He could've said whatever he wanted. As long as it got me to SJ, I would agree. When he mentioned my baby, I tuned in just in time to hear him tell me that I would be able to go downstairs to see him.

I couldn't contain my excitement, knowing I was actually

going to be able to see and touch the little guy who had been kicking me for the last two months. Tisha came in with a wheelchair and helped me into another gown to cover my backside before she and Shai got me into the chair since I was unsteady on my feet.

My mama decided to stay back in the room since she'd just come from seeing him, while Shai came with me. The whole ride down to the NICU, I was a ball of nerves, bouncing between being excited and scared. But once Tisha wheeled me into the room and I laid eyes on my baby, that all went away.

He was palm sized, only weighing one pound and a few ounces. His body appeared almost translucent and extremely fragile, with tubes sticking out of him. Tisha wheeled me to the sink in the room to wash my hands and then over to his incubator. I just watched his chest rising and falling for a minute before I got the courage to stick my hands in the little holes and touch him. His skin was just as soft as it looked, and his fingers were too tiny for me to pick up comfortably, so I opted to just rub them.

"Hi, baby Shai. I'm your mommy!" I gushed quietly, unable to stop myself from grinning as I took in his features. It was too early to tell who he favored more, but that didn't matter because he was just beautiful to me.

"You did good, love." Shai came up behind me, giving my shoulders a squeeze as he kissed the top of my head.

That had the waterworks starting again because had I done good? Our son was laid in an incubator and being fed through a tube because he hadn't been able to finish developing in my belly like he should've. I don't think anyone understood how much of a failure not being able to carry a baby to term could make you feel like. Even though Shai Jr. had made it out, he wasn't in the clear, and I was going to feel like dying if he didn't make it. Closing my eyes, I said a silent prayer for God to keep my baby alive and healthy.

I stayed for as long as I could, just staring at him in awe until Tisha finally came back and said that I needed to eat. At first, I refused, not wanting to miss any moments with him, but when she told me about the requirements of my discharge, I reluctantly allowed her to wheel me back to my room, only perking up when she told me I could come back after a couple hours of rest.

I thought for sure I wasn't going to be tired after eating, especially since I was still bubbling with energy from seeing my little man, but as soon as I ate the last spoonful of pudding, my eyes drifted closed.

I heard Shai's voice before I saw him, even though he was talking lowly in an effort not to wake me up. When I opened my eyes, he had his back to me, and I could almost see the tension rolling off him as he hissed into the phone. "I don't give a fuck Kendra's crazy ass needs to be in somebody's psych ward! If she's not in cuffs leaving this hospital, she gon' leave in a body bag. April's lucky I can't press charges against her ass for making Zuri go into labor with her bullshit! Don't call me back with this shit! I'm tryna spend time with my woman and son!"

I'd really forgotten all about the reason we were there in the first place because Shai Jr. was dominating my thoughts, but his conversation instantly piqued my interest. Going into labor had prevented me from finding out why Kadeem had actually called me and my mama up to the hospital, but it obviously had something to do with my sister, judging from Shai's conversation. Hell, I'd never gotten the chance to find out what *he* was doing at the hospital, and now I was irritated.

He hung up, cursing under his breath, but his face relaxed once he turned around and saw my eyes on him. I was sure my face showed my confusion, but he rushed over, asking me everything under the sun without explaining what I'd just heard.

"What's Kendra doing up here?" I quizzed, dodging the kiss he tried to give me. I wasn't necessarily mad at him, but I wasn't letting him skate past what he'd said. His shoulders drooped instantly, and I could tell he didn't want to tell me. Bucking my eyes, I motioned for him to answer, and he released a heavy sigh.

"Yesterday, Kendra drove her car through my restaurant.

That's why we were all up here already because I wanted to make sure I could press charges against her ass if she made it out okay." My brows shot up at that because I wasn't expecting to hear anything like that had happened. I thought at most she'd tried to kill herself, and in a way, she had, but this was crazier than anything I could've imagined. He went through the events of the day before, horrifying me even more as I got the details.

As sad as it was, I couldn't help thinking that my father had to be totally demented to have called me to the hospital after what Kendra had done. To know that after all the damage she'd caused, she was walking away with a broken leg and concussion was crazy as hell. It didn't matter what happened to her; it was obvious she wasn't going to let this thing with Shai and me go. She was giving Lifetime Network psycho vibes, and I was with Shai that she needed to be locked up in somebody's padded room.

"Don't worry, love, I'll make sure they handle her," Shai asserted, seeing the concern on my face.

The last time he'd said that I wasn't sure if I believed him, but something about the look in his eyes let me know this was different.

SEVYN

"Nope, get that thing away from me!" I fussed, wiggling away from Zaakir and his hard dick. He'd just gotten out of the shower after fucking me half the afternoon, but his dick was already hard and tenting underneath his royal blue towel. "I'm tryna make it to the hospital to see Zuri before visiting hours are over." I continued moving around and getting dressed as he came at me again, latching onto my waist. A low moan escaped when he pressed himself into me, but I remembered the mission and shoved his ass off.

"Man, stop playin' with me, Sev. I'm tryna send yo' fine ass off with a smile on yo' face, and you playin'."

I laughed, and his grown ass had the nerve to have his face balled up like I was really getting on his nerves or some shit.

"Seeing my nephew and best friend is gon' put a smile on my face. Plus, I got flashbacks to hold me over anyway."

"I'll let you see the video I got of Zuri's mama beating up Kendra's mama," he offered, raising his eyebrows with his sneaky ass.

This was the first time I'd heard about a video, and I can't lie; I was salty he hadn't told me already. I froze and narrowed my eyes at him.

"What video?"

"The one I recorded, muthafuckas. You tryna drain these balls to see it or naw?" he said with the most serious expression as he grabbed his dick.

"Not you tryna bargain with dick. Petty ass."

He stepped back with a shrug. "Call it what you want, but I know you don't wanna miss the way Ms. Zora knocked that hoe's shit loose."

"Mmm, you got a point," I admitted begrudgingly. "I'm only givin' yo' ass some head tho, 'cause I'm not tryna waste time taking a whole 'nother shower." I poked him in the chest with narrowed eyes, and he smirked, knowing he'd won me over.

Rolling my eyes, I dropped to my knees and swallowed his dick whole. I planned to put all my extra skills to use to get him to nut quick, but the way he was hissing and moaning, I couldn't help getting turned on myself. He held onto my head with both hands, forcing my eyes up. The look of pleasure on his face had my hand slipping down the front of my jeans, which was no easy task. My fingers were instantly drenched, and Zaakir's lids lowered when he realized what I was doing.

"Let me taste that, Sev." He licked his lips and leaned forward so I could reach his mouth.

"Mmm!" I whimpered, mouth still full of dick as my clit throbbed from the way he was sucking my fingers.

"You want this dick up in you, baby?" His voice was husky, and I nodded with a moan. I definitely wanted to feel him at that point. "Come bend yo' ass over," he demanded, pulling away and helping me to my feet.

I struggled to get my jeans unbuttoned and tossed my hair over my shoulder as I bent over the closest thing to me, which happened to be my dresser. My pants only made it just below my ass cheeks before he forced a deeper arch in my back and slammed into me.

"Ahhh, fuck! Zaakiiiiir!" My eyes fluttered as waves of pleasure hit me like a Mack truck. I never thought I'd get so much satisfaction while being constricted to a single position, but damn if I didn't feel my juices leaking down my leg like water.

"I swear I could live in this pussy, girl! Damn!" he grumbled, wrapping a hand around my hair and yanking my head back as he continued to deliver powerful strokes.

"Deeper, bae!" My mouth fell open, and my eyes rolled when he honored my request, slowing down and grinding so I felt every inch. He leaned forward, pressing his chest into my back. That only added more pressure, giving him access to my G-spot.

"You finna let me fill this pussy, Sev?" His voice was strained as he buried his face in my neck, licking my flesh, and my legs damn near gave out.

"Yes! Mmmhm! Yes! I'm bouta cum, Zaakir, shiiit!" My body tingled all over, and my stomach grew tight. I erupted within seconds, body quivering, head spinning, and knees weak to the point that I lost the ability to hold myself up.

"Fuuuck!"

Zaakir slipped an arm around my waist to hold me up as he came himself. I could feel him pulsing, filling me up until his body slumped against mine. I don't know how much time passed before I felt like I could actually control my own body, and I went to push him off me. "Move, Zaakir! You get on my nerves!"

"Yo' freaky ass wanted me in this pussy just as bad as I wanted to be in it. Now, be still and let my damn kids settle down in there," his crazy ass demanded, tightening the grip he had on me, and I cracked up laughing.

"Boy! I'm not bouta play with you! Let me go, so I can go wash my ass!"

"So, now you tryna drown my kids? That's fucked up." He had the nerve to sound genuinely hurt, but I couldn't even take his dumb ass seriously. "You a fucked up individual, Sev." He finally let me go, snatching his towel off the floor.

"And you a crazy ass individual, so it makes sense that we're together." I shimmied the rest of the way out of my jeans and panties before following him into the bathroom.

"Don't be tryna say sweet shit now. I'm still mad at yo' ass," he grumbled petulantly and turned to cut on the shower.

"Really, Zaakir? You're being childish right now 'cause I know you ain't really mad." I eyed him, knowing he was full of shit. "Nigga, you is not mad about kids that don't exist for real."

"Man, come get yo' ass in the shower, so we can go see my nephew." He climbed in first, and against my better judgment, I joined him, thinking it would cut the time in half, but somehow, I ended up bouncing on his dick with my legs in the creases of his arms.

We didn't leave until two whole hours later, making us even more late since I still needed to stop and get some flowers and stuff. When I finally made it to Zuri's room, I had tears in my eyes. Although I knew Shai had her one hundred percent, I couldn't help feeling like I wasn't there for her like I should've been. We were besties, more like sisters than anything, and I never wanted her to feel like I wasn't doing my job.

"Biiiitch, I missed you!" I gushed, running over, but I stopped short once I was within arm's reach. "Can we? Is it okay for me to hug you? 'Cause I'm not tryna hurt you."

"Girl, get over here. I missed yo' crazy tail self, too!"

"Good, 'cause I'm not going nowhere until they discharge you. I already got my bags packed," I let her know, tapping my Neverfull bag with a grin. "Sorry, Shai."

"*Sorry, Shai,* my ass! Naw, you a goddamn lie! You ain't staying nowhere with yo' sneaky ass. I should've known you had more than yo' wallet and shit in that big ass purse!" Zaakir appeared at my side, setting her balloons and flowers on the table but handing her the gift bag we'd brought even as he talked shit.

"Shut up, Zaakir! If I said I'm staying with my bestie, that's what I'm doing!" I stuck my tongue out at him while he talked shit under his breath.

"Aww, thanks, y'all!" She beamed, looking beautiful despite her hair being all over her head. Motherhood suited her, and I couldn't help feeling a little down, but I hid it well. "Are y'all going downstairs to see SJ?"

"Of course. I just wanted to stop here first so you didn't get all jelly, but that's my next stop." I'd been trying to keep my excitement bottled up, but the mention of the baby had me unable to hide it.

"You're so damn phony." She scoffed, narrowing her eyes at me, feigning attitude.

"Awww, it's okay, bookie. I'm staying with you, though."

"That's what yo' ass think."

Ignoring Zaakir's little side comments, I promised I'd be back soon. I left her to look through her gifts and headed down to the NICU, where they said SJ was, with Zaakir's ass on my heels. For as childish as he always was, Zaakir's whole energy shifted once we reached the floor with the babies, and he grabbed my hand in his. We walked together to the room where a big glass displayed the babies. It wasn't hard to spot baby A'santi's name outside his little crib. He was tiny, with a head full of black curls, and he was wearing only a doll-sized diaper. I had to refrain from tapping the glass, even though I knew he wasn't alert enough to look my way.

Despite how happy I was to see him, my thoughts instantly went to my own baby. I wondered if it would've been a boy or girl and who it would've favored more. I didn't realize I was crying until my tears landed on my hand. Silently, Zaakir hugged me from behind and pressed a kiss to the top of my head, already sensing what I needed in that moment. I couldn't lie; it was the most comforting thing ever. Moments like this made me love him more.

SHAI

It was the day they were releasing Zuri from the hospital, and I already knew she was going to feel some type of way. Neither of us wanted to leave SJ at the hospital, and if I could've rented a room for her in the hospital so she could stay, I would've, but they had already told my ass no. I was down in her room, grabbing the last of her things while she said goodbye to baby SJ. It had only been four days, but my little man was going strong, and the doctors had nothing but good things to say about his progress.

By the time I made it back upstairs, they'd returned Zuri to her room. Her mama and Sevyn sat with her while the nurse went over her aftercare instructions and gave her the discharge papers. I already knew she'd have to take it easy for a few weeks, which was why I made sure to have her packed up so she didn't have to worry about it. Since the restaurant was closed until the repairs were done, I'd be able to be at her beck and call until she was at one hundred percent.

"Okay, again, it's been a pleasure taking care of you, girl, and I hope you have a speedy recovery. Make sure you call me too, girl," the nurse Tisha said, bending to give Zuri another hug before saying her goodbyes to us and leaving. She'd been with her since the day she was admitted, so they'd grown quite a bond to the point that she'd even come to visit her on her day off. I watched Sevyn's facial expression sour at the gesture, but she quickly straightened her face when she caught me looking.

"Damn, she took long enough!" Ms. Zora huffed, opening the little duffle bag she had as soon as Tish stepped out of the room. "I'm convinced her ass was just in here tryna cock block." She moved around the room, hurriedly emptying drawers and cabinets while Sevyn cackled, and Zuri tried hard to keep it in.

"Ma, that's enough. You gon' have us banned from every hospital and doctor's office." She tried to sound stern, even though I knew she was struggling not to laugh for fear of the pain she knew she'd feel.

I was just puzzled about what was even going on, but I wasn't about to step to Ms. Zora after the way I saw her beating on April. As if I'd summoned her, my phone vibrated in my hand, but when I saw it was her, I shoved that shit down in my pocket. She'd been trying to get me to drop the charges against Kendra, but that shit was dead. As far as I knew, she was still downstairs, handcuffed to her bed until she was in good enough condition to go to jail.

"You ready, love?" I moved behind Zuri's wheelchair and grabbed the handles.

"I'm waiting on Swiper," she cracked, and even I had to laugh, making her mama mug us hard.

"Ha ha, everybody got jokes, but you won't be laughing when you need something from out of Swiper's bag." She shook the bag in her hands before setting it on the bed to zip it closed. Once she finished, she tossed it over her shoulder and strutted to the door, holding it open like she hadn't just cleaned out the room.

I went ahead and pushed Zuri out, shaking my head at their asses. A chorus of well wishes and goodbyes rang out as we passed the nurse's station. Everywhere Zuri went, she made friends, and it was just a testament to how beautiful she was inside and out, no matter what she went through.

"Did you make sure you got everything, Ms. Zora?" Tisha called out, giving her a knowing look.

Zuri's mama had no shame as she patted the side of her bag. "Sure did!"

I shook my head and continued to the elevator because their asses were all crazy as hell. When we made it downstairs, I helped Zuri into the passenger side and ran around to hop in the driver's seat. I could already tell she was feeling some type of way about having to leave. She looked up at the hospital and sighed all dramatically, so I lifted her hand in mine, giving it a squeeze before kissing the back of it.

"You wanna stop and get some food before we head home? Anything you want," I offered with raised eyebrows, making her head finally turn away from the window.

"I'm not pregnant anymore, so food isn't the only thing on my mind anymore." She made a face at me, and I shrugged.

"My bad."

"I could go for some Pepe's, though." She rolled her eyes, trying to sound nonchalant despite her damn near drooling.

"Pepe's do sound good," I admitted, heading that way.

After I grabbed the food, I headed to the new house, watching Zuri's face when I finally pulled onto our block, but she was too busy stuffing her face.

"What we doin' here? I thought we were going to your house?" she asked when I stopped the car in the driveway to wait for the garage to open.

"We're here 'cause this is home. Besides, I already emptied out my crib, and it's been on the market for a couple weeks. Yours will be too in the next week."

"You packed up my house too?"

"Yeah, man, I didn't want you coming home and having to worry about that. You just need to rest, and when you feel up to it, maybe you can take yo' new car for a spin," I said, throwing her off.

Her brows dipped as I nodded toward the garage, where a rose gold 2024 Lexus GX sat with a big red bow across the hood.

"S-Shai, is that me-my mine?" She asked wide eyed, unable to form a complete sentence.

"Of course. You gon' need some new shit to be ridin' in with our young king. This yo' push gift. What y'all be sayin'? You gon' be killin' hoes this summer." I laughed, but I was dead serious. I was trying to make sure my woman was riding clean. "What you waitin' on, love? Let's go check that shit out.

She wiped the fresh tears from her face and moved to open her door. I was right there to help her out, and I walked beside her until she was at the driver's door.

After I helped her behind the wheel, she looked around frantically, unsure of what to touch first, when I put the keys in her hands. The inside was decked out in the same rose gold and black as the outside, with her name stitched on the headrests.

"Oh, my God! I love it! Thank you, baby!" She swooned, still crying. "I gotta call Sevyn and tell her!" She pulled her phone out and FaceTimed Sevyn, already bouncing around in her seat before it finally connected. "Biiiiitch, look what Shai just surprised me with!" The way she was moving the phone around, I figured she had flipped the camera around to show her, and I could hear Sevyn's loud ass screaming.

"Okay, baby daddy! Look at you comin' through with a fire ass custom whip for my girl! I see you!" she hooted.

I could tell she was genuinely excited for my baby, and I loved that. At first, I was looking at her sideways after the bomb Unc dropped on us, but me and Zaakir had been looking into that shit, and not only did she get a bad deal from her nigga, but she got one from the police too. Sevyn was thorough, though, and she made sure to keep Zuri out of the way, which really gave her ass points in my book. The only problem was that she gave the wrong people her loyalty before she met Zaakir. If I knew my cousin, though, he was going to match her energy and make sure she came out unscathed.

"Damn, Zaakir, why you don't never do nothin' sweet like this for me? I like Lexus' too."

"Maaaan, give me that! Aye, Shai, why you always tryna outdo me, causing problems in my house and shit!" Zaakir came on the line, talking shit as usual, and they started going back and forth arguing.

I ignored his silly ass and put my attention on Zuri, giving her a quick kiss.

"I'ma run yo' shit in the crib and come back to walk you in," I let her know. "Wait for me to come back, Zuri. I ain't playin'," I warned before walking off to grab her things out of the trunk.

After two trips, I had brought everything up to our bedroom and rushed back downstairs to get Zuri before she tried to be superwoman and come up herself. This house was different than either of our old ones, and it would be a lot harder for her to get up to the bedroom. Shit, even I was winded.

I came back just in time to catch her ass locking up the truck from outside it. "Mmmhmm, I got yo' ass!" I came up behind her, and she damn near jumped out of her skin. "Didn't I tell you to wait for me?"

She smiled, shrugging innocently as I got closer. "I mean, I did. Just out here."

"Slick ass," I teased, carefully lifting her up bridal style.

She took in the décor as I carried her upstairs, amazed that I was able to get it all done in such a short amount of time, but she hadn't seen the real surprise yet. When we finally made it upstairs, I stopped at the door just before our bedroom, and she looked at me with wide, misty eyes.

"You didn't."

Instead of responding, I pushed the door open, and she gasped, taking in every inch of SJ's room. Since we found out it was a boy, she'd decided on a blue, gray, and white theme. We'd already ordered a lot of his big furniture, so there wasn't much left for me to have done besides painting and setting it all up. I set her on her feet so she could check everything out on her own and watched her move around, touching everything.

"You did so... good." Her voice cracked as she started crying again.

"It'll be okay, love. He'll be home soon," I let her know and sent up a silent prayer that I wasn't lying to her.

SEVYN

Since Tramel was dead and Rome was missing, Detective Hill had been on one and pressing me harder. With each day that passed, he was threatening to come and snatch my life away. I was trying to trust Zaakir when he said he had me, but Hill was beginning to make me nervous. For the longest, I'd been looking out for myself and everybody else, so it felt strange to let Zaakir handle everything. Shit, a part of me wanted to start making moves on my own in the event that this whole thing collapsed on me, but then I'd think about how Zaakir had always looked out and decided against it.

"You okay, bitch? You been over there just staring off into space and shit for the last ten minutes." I came out of my thoughts, and Tyrese was staring at me curiously.

"I'm good, just thinkin' about some shit," I lied and started shuffling the papers on my desk. The last thing I wanted was for him to worry because scared people did stupid shit. I couldn't afford for him to go trying to make a side deal because he thought that was his only choice. He side eyed me, so I forced out a laugh to put him at ease. "For real, I was just thinking about all the shit I have to do today. I'm tired just running down the list."

He clicked his tongue and waved. "Girl, same. That's why I

do all my running around on my days off. I'd fuck around and wouldn't get shit done if I had to do it after we leave here."

"Lucky you, bitch. I don't have no days off," I chided, feigning an attitude.

"That's because you won't take none. The only time you've been away from this place was when you were in the hospital and when it was shut down because of yo' trifling husband."

He was right. This shop was my baby, and I couldn't fathom being away from it. With the way business was going, I probably wouldn't be taking any more time off either. Plus, there was no telling when Detective Hill would come back, trying to shut me down again. Campbell was at least working to get me out of the deal I'd made, which was all that was fucking things up since Tramel was dead. I wasn't worried about Rome because, without the brains, he wasn't a real threat.

"Well, now that I'm a widow, once I get this shit all straightened out, I can take a vacation with my man." I shrugged.

"Oooh, a vacation sounds good, but I'm thinking more of a girl's trip than a baecation. Just think about all us girls on the beach, twerking in white sand, on a yacht, twerking like we in the Rock the Boat video. You know, real cute shit."

"That does sound good." I couldn't lie; that shit did sound good after everything we'd been dealing with in the last few months. I could already see myself lying on the beach in a cute ass bikini with a drink in my hand. The only problem was that I couldn't even plan for that shit until this case was completely closed.

"Period!" he cosigned, getting even more excited. "If you want, I could set that up and—"

"Have us coming home to warrants, fool! We can't leave the city while the police still doing their lil' investigation, but as soon as they do, we out this bitch!"

"Damn, you right. Oooh, I hate Tramel ass!"

"Don't we all," I grumbled, finally finished with the stuff I was working on.

I put everything away and snatched up my coat to leave. It was the end of the night, and as usual, Tyrese and I were the last two there. I'd been on my feet for the last twelve hours, and I couldn't wait to get home and relax in a tub of Epsom salt.

Like he'd been doing since my return, Tyrese walked me out to my car while I shot Zaakir another text. He'd been available all day, but for the last couple of hours, he was MIA. All I was trying to do was find out if I was going to his house or if he was coming to mine, but his sudden disappearance was going to be the reason I just took my ass home.

"Awwww!" Tyrese gushed.

My head snapped up to see Zaakir leaning against a matte black Lexus just like Zuri's and holding out the key toward me. He was trying to look serious, but he couldn't stop his lips from spreading into a grin.

"Gone 'head let it out," his cocky ass said, and I released the scream I'd been holding in as I ran over.

"Oh, my God, baby! Thank you!" I jumped in his arms, giving him a sloppy kiss that had my clit throbbing. That fast, I was ready to take his fine ass down in the parking lot, but Tyrese cleared his throat loudly, reminding me of his presence.

"Damn, Sev. Baby, all I gotta do is buy yo' ass somethin' for you to be all up on a nigga? Noted." He pulled away, grinning sexily, and I wiggled out of his arms.

"Swear you know how to ruin a moment." Scoffing, I gave him a light shove, and he caught my arm, pulling me back to him. His hands found my ass and squeezed, biting his lip.

"Naw, I like when you like this, all happy and shit. For real, I'm just happy to be the reason." My insides melted from the look he was giving. "Gone 'head check out yo' new truck, baby." He gave me a quick kiss before letting me go, and I snatched the keys out of his hand. Tyrese had already found his way inside and was gushing over the features when I climbed in.

"Okaaaay Zaaaakiiiiiir, you got my bitch right!" he acknowledged when Zaakir leaned in my doorway, and pride was obvious on his face.

He definitely had a lot to be proud of because he'd done his big one. Leather peanut butter bucket seats with rhinestone accents, a panoramic sunroof, and he even already had a little air freshener in there with one of my favorite scents.

"You drive this, and I'll drive yo' old joint to the crib," Zaakir said, and I pulled him to me by his shirt, kissing him again.

"Okay." I placed my old keys in his hand, and I couldn't help simpering as I watched him walk away.

Tyrese snickered beside me. "You got it bad, bitch. Nigga detox my ass." He shook his head.

"You don't know my life!" my lying ass quickly denied, only making him laugh more. "Get out, so I can drive home to my *nigga*." I shooed his aggravating ass away, and he threw his hands up in surrender, still laughing.

"Okay, bitch. I'll let you get on home, but you better make sure you suck the skin off that nigga's dick tonight!"

"You already know I plan to!" I nodded, slapping hands with him before he finally climbed out, and I pulled off to do just that.

A couple days later, I was leaving the mall after grabbing some more stuff for SJ. It was really supposed to be a quick run to grab myself the new Jordans, but when I saw some in infant sizes, I couldn't resist getting him a pair. Then I figured that he'd need some more clothes to go with them, and two hours later, I was leaving with bags in each hand. I'd just put my stuff in the trunk when I heard my name called, and I immediately cringed. I knew Detective Hill's voice anywhere. I contemplated whether I could make a run for it before deciding not to even try it as I heard his loud ass shoes sliding across the concrete.

"How you keep finding me?" I huffed, folding my arms when he finally stopped in front of me.

"This is just a coincidence. I'm actually here getting my daughter the new Jordans." He shrugged, eyes landing on my truck. "This new?"

"Yeah, I—"

"I'm just curious on how you can afford this when your shop is only bringing in regular money now... or is it?" I should've known he was going to be on his bullshit, as usual. First, he accused me of having something to do with Tramel's death, and now he thought I still had access to drugs. At this rate, his ass wasn't ever gon' be lead detective.

"You ain't heard of a car note?"

He cocked his head as he looked me over like he wasn't sure he believed me, even though it made perfect sense. I was really starting to think it didn't matter what I said; he'd always assume I was guilty. He couldn't have any other cases because he was on me like I was a big fish when I wasn't even a regular sized one.

"Car note. That's a good one."

"Look, what do you want, man? You keep popping up and callin' me like you don't got no other cases you could be focusing on until I get you what you want." I sized him up, narrowing my eyes when I got to his face and saw a smirk there. "You got a crush on me or somethin'? 'Cause I can tell you now, I'd *never* fuck with a nigga with a badge." I sneered with my nose turned up, wiping the grin right off his face. I hated niggas who tried to take advantage of their position over somebody, and that's exactly what it seemed like he was on.

"So, you only like thugs? That's understandable, but I'd hardly call Zaakir A'santi a thug." His eyes lit up, seeing my discomfort at the mention of Zaakir.

It didn't take a rocket scientist to figure out that he only knew of him from his stalking tendencies. If he didn't consider him a thug, though, then maybe he didn't know any of his business despite his meddling ways.

"Tuh, I said I don't fuck with police. I ain't never say I only wanted thugs. Meaning, I'd fuck with almost anybody before I scraped the bottom of the barrel." I had to stop myself from calling his ass a goofy because I didn't want to offend him any more than I already had.

A man's ego was fragile as fuck, and even more so when it was bruised. I wasn't trying to find out what he was capable of when something like that happened to him. His face darkened, and he took a threatening step my way. "I'd watch how the fuck you talk to me, Sevyn. It's not like you have very many options right now, and I can lock yo' little black ass up whenever I want to. I'm the only reason you're still out and able to sleep in your own bed and make money in that little ass shop! Don't you ever forget that!" His mad ass poked my chest before disappearing toward the mall. The whole interaction had me shaken up, and I couldn't wait to tell Zaakir.

ZAAKIR

When Sevyn came to the crib and told me about that weird ass detective, I was livid. For one, he knew my name, and although he hadn't found shit out about me, that didn't mean he wasn't going to stop since he found out. For two, it sounded like he was threatening her, and I really didn't like that shit.

I left her at the house and immediately hit up Elle so I could find out everything she could get on Hill. I was barely off the block by the time she got back to me with his entire life, but most importantly, his address. Speeding up, I hit a U-turn and headed in that direction, not realizing she was still on the phone.

"Z, what do you think you're gonna go and do? That nigga a cop, a highly decorated detective," she stressed. "You can't just go touch him like y'all do everybody else, and you damn sure shouldn't be doin' it cause of that girl."

My face balled up at the way she was talking. It wasn't like she hadn't expressed her dislike for Sevyn on multiple occasions, especially after she found out she was working with the police, but I didn't appreciate her tone. She was talking like she had a say so in anything I did or who I was fucking with, and that wasn't part of her job description.

I sucked my teeth and hit the next turn I was supposed to. "You trippin', Elle. I didn't call you for no life advice. I hit yo' ass up for info, that's it. All that other shit you sayin' is unnecessary. I'm straight over here."

"I just think—"

I hung up on her ass as she was talking because I didn't have shit else to say, and I wasn't trying to hear shit either. She was crazy if she thought I was letting Sevyn go and even crazier for thinking I wasn't gonna check that nigga behind her just because he was a cop.

I wasn't even surprised when Shai's number popped up on the screen next. Of course, she called his ass, trying to snitch on me. Instead of answering and having to hear his mouth, I let the shit go to voicemail. I already knew all he'd try to do was talk me out of it, and I wasn't doing that. Detective Hill was gon' die tonight!

Almost an hour later, I was driving by his house, scoping the scene. According to the shit Elle had sent, his ass didn't have a wife and kids, and his neighborhood was shit. I could understand why his ass was so mad, having to live in the type of shithole he resided in and seeing a woman like Sevyn doing it big, but that was no excuse to be harassing her the way he was. It couldn't have been because he loved his job so damn much, that was for sure.

After I drove past a couple of times to make sure there weren't any cameras and was confident that his shit was still, I parked on the next block and cut through a couple yards until I was standing at his back door. Just like when I'd left, all the lights were off. I got my gun ready before pulling on my ski mask, but the sound of footsteps had me raising it in that direction.

"Put that shit down, nigga. It's me!" Shai hissed, and I cursed under my breath.

"Nigga, I almost just shot yo' stupid ass! Fuck you sneakin' up on me for?"

A dog barked, making us both crouch under the window just in case somebody was coming or looking at our asses. The moment passed, and once I was sure nobody was coming, I pushed his ass, almost making him fall off his feet.

"Fuck you doin' here?"

"Tryna keep yo' dumb ass from goin' to prison!" he snapped, pushing me back.

We stared each other down, and I really could've knocked his meddling ass out if it wasn't for where we were.

"Man, I'm gon' slap the shit out Elle. She run her mouth too fuckin' much! Bitch think she a homie, and her ass a fuckin' employee."

"This shit ain't Elle's fault, nigga. Yo' dumb ass the one out here bouta get us all fucked up!" I heard movement at the same time that Shai did, and we both pointed our guns, only to see my pop's old ass.

"Nigga, what the fuck yo' old ass doin' out here?" I hissed when he was close enough. "Y'all niggas actin' like this a family reunion or some shit!" Elle's ass had called everybody, thinking she was helping when she could've gotten all our black asses locked up.

"I came to stop yo' goofy ass from doin' some stupid shit and gettin' caught up!" I mugged his old ass and resisted the urge to kick his ass in his shin.

Him and Shai were getting on my fucking nerves, and I swore I wasn't messin' with Elle's ass no more. I'd fuck around and do my own investigation or have Shai contact her whenever we needed some shit I couldn't get.

"Fuck both y'all!" I huffed, standing up.

They did the same, still trying to talk me down, but I ignored them and looked for an unlocked window. He had windows all around that shit, but clearly, he didn't check them because, by the time I got around to the dining room, I found one that slid right up. It was quiet as fuck, too, so I knew it wasn't going to alert anybody once I climbed through it. I was halfway in when they came behind me, hissing for my ass to get down, but they wouldn't jeopardize us getting caught by doing too much.

Once I was in, I stood to my full height, testing the weight of his raggedy ass floors for any squeaking. When I didn't hear any, I moved deeper inside. My eyes quickly adjusted to the dark, and I could see that the living and dining rooms were open to each other while the kitchen was behind a wall. I peeked around the corner, and once I made sure the coast was clear, I turned to check the rest of the house and right into Shai's ass.

Since we were inside, I didn't curse his ass out like I wanted to; I just sent a nasty mug his way. If they hadn't been on my back, blocking, I would've already double-tapped that nigga and been out. Motioning for them to be quiet, I headed down a short hall and listened intently. I could make out the sounds of loud snoring and knew that's where Hill was. Luckily, I didn't have to go too far because his was the first room I came upon, and his ass was alone.

Grinning, I flipped the light on and stepped completely into the room. With light bathing the area, I was able to see the multiple liquor and pill bottles that littered his dresser. It was no wonder his ass was acting the way he was. His ass was 'bout high and drunk all the time.

"Aye, this shit might work in our favor." Shai nodded, eying the shit too.

I rolled my eyes. His ass was always trying to take the fun out of shit.

"I see where you goin', nephew. That would be better, but you gon' have to make sure you don't hit his ass or no shit like that," Casa said, giving me a look like I'd be the one to fuck it up.

"Man, ain't nobody gon' hit this nigga! Even I know white people bruise easy as fuck." I sucked my teeth, and all our heads whipped toward the bed when Hill moved, groaning.

He must have felt us watching him because his eyes slowly drifted open, and he went to reach, but I quickly put a stop to that.

"Aht aht, nigga. Leave that shit where it's at."

With three guns pointed his way, he was smart enough to give it up. He backed up to the headboard with his hands raised as his eyes bounced between us frantically.

"You're Shai A'santi, and you're Casanova." He looked fearfully from Shai to Casa, and then his gaze landed on me. "Zaakir?" He tilted his head, trying hard to see through my mask, so I lifted it to the top of my head and smirked.

"Yeah, it's me, muthafucka. Surprised?" I hated the stupid ass look on his face, even though it was warranted. He should've definitely been scared.

"Wh-what are you doing in m-my house?"

Keeping my gun on him, I shared a look with Shai. "I'm here to see you, nigga. I thought you wanted to talk or something since you had so much to say to my girl about me." I craned my neck, staring at him in amusement.

"S-Sevyn?"

"Yeah, muthafuckas, S-Sevyn." His eyes widened, and he started breathing heavily as Casa snorted.

"This nigga here so whipped."

"Man, fuck you, Casa!" Shooting a look his way, I was met with the same mug, but that shit wasn't moving me.

"Look, if this is about the case, m-maybe we can work something out!" Hill's voice was high-pitched and wild as he tried to get our attention.

Even though I had no intention of entertaining that shit, I motioned for him to continue. The more he talked, the more hope appeared on his face. Once he was finished, I waited a few seconds to speak as if I was thinking.

"Actually, I think I got a better idea. Why don't you grab that pill bottle over there?" The request had his face twisting, even as he went to do what I said. "Now, open that shit up and take 'em. I'll even let you wash 'em down with that Jameson over there." I grinned as his face fell in horror.

"You... you want me to kill myself?" he balked, looking at Shai and then at Casa like they would help him.

"I mean, you wanna kill yo' self too. You're out here trying to revive a case that's dead by setting up an innocent woman to take the fall for her piece of shit husband." I shrugged and folded one hand over the other in front of me.

"Sounds about white!" Shai chimed, making me and Casa's eyes swing his way.

"Nigga, what?"

"Yo' ass half white, nigga! Stop talkin' 'bout yo' white half like that."

"Y'all muthafuckas childish as fuck. You yo' daddy's son like a muthafucka!" he grumbled with an attitude.

"Can we just finish this shit? I was in the middle of something." Casa moved, taking a seat on the edge of his long dresser with his gun in hand and resting against his leg.

I decided not to point out how I hadn't called either of their asses to come ride with me, but I left it alone. Honestly, I was ready to get the shit over with anyway, and I knew Hill was going to beg, plead, and some more shit before he finally took the pills.

"Man, get his service gun." I nodded to Shai, who went over and quickly found it under his pillow. It was going to be my plan B just in case he did too much and I got tired of playing around.

"Wait, I—" Hill's eyes damn near popped out of his head, but I quickly cut him off.

"I'll let you pick yo' poison. Either it's gon' be the pills or the gun. Actually, it probably makes more sense for an officer to use the gun. Gone 'head write yo' note." I pointed my gun toward the pen and small pad next to him on the dresser. He hesitated before taking his time to lean over and get it, looking up at me expectantly once they were in his hands. "Good, now write exactly what I tell you. Nothin' more, nothin' less."

"Actually, let me get this part, cuz," Shai said, and I shrugged.

I wasn't even going to do all this originally, so if he wanted to do it, that was cool. I just wanted his ass dead. He stood over the detective and gave him a full script that I had to admit sounded like the type of note that somebody about to kill themselves would write. His crazy ass was nodding and shit-like a schoolteacher, and when Hill finally finished it to his satisfaction, the nigga patted him on top of the head. Giving a nod, he had him set it back on the side table amongst the other shit there and then moved to the opposite side of the bed with his gun in hand. Hill followed him with his eyes, and so did I because I didn't know what that nigga was doing.

"Fuck you goin' over there for?"

"Cause he left-handed, nigga, damn! I know what the fuck I'm doin'!" He mugged me, and I had to admit that shit was smart as hell.

I definitely hadn't thought about which hand the nigga would use to off himself. Throwing my hands up, I motioned for him to proceed while Hill began to beg. Shai hit him with a single bullet midsentence that had his ass slumping to the other side of the bed. He wasted no time cleaning his prints off the gun and pressing it into the detective's hand.

"See how easy that was? I keep tellin' yo' impatient ass to let me handle shit." He grumbled, wiping down anything else in the room we might have touched.

"How 'bout fuck you." I followed him out of the room with Casa coming behind me, wiping anything either of us might've missed.

I let him talk his shit because they had come through in the clutch, and within minutes, we were back out the same way we'd come in and headed to our cars.

ZURI

Three months had passed since I had my baby, and he was improving every day. He'd already gained four and a half pounds and had been able to drink from my breasts for the last month. His features had come in, and he looked just like Shai, from his curly hair down to his little lips. He'd gotten a little color to him, too, even though he was still light bright, taking after his daddy in that department as well. It was like I had no parts in his making, but I didn't mind it. I was just happy he was here and healthy.

It was time for me to go for my visit with him, and I double-checked his diaper bag to make sure I had a few outfits for him to change into since he threw up more than other babies due to stomach issues. I really couldn't wait until the day they told me I could bring him home. It was going to be soon, though, because he was doing so well. Until then, I was going to keep going up to the hospital daily.

I smelled Shai before I saw him, and butterflies danced in my belly like it was the first time I'd ever been in his presence. He came up behind me, wrapping his arms around my waist and kissing my neck.

"You look thick as hell in these. Got me ready to put another baby in you right now. Damn!" Groaning, he pressed himself against me, and I giggled, caressing his head. "You laughin', but SJ needs a lil' brother or sister." I could already feel him hardening against my ass just from the thought of impregnating me, but the joke was on him.

After having Shai Jr., I had the doctor give me the shot. I knew I wanted more babies, but I wanted my son home and at one hundred percent before I even thought about carrying again. Plus, getting over a c-section was no easy feat, and I'd just gotten my shape back, so he would have to wait.

"SJ doesn't even know what a younger sibling is, so I know he don't care to have one. And you, baby, can definitely wait since you're not the one who had to have stitches last time," I pointed out, and he hummed in response, sucking my earlobe into his mouth.

"Ayite, then I'll just pull out." He moved his hands up my body and lightly grabbed my breast. Even if he wasn't convincing me, his hands and mouth damn sure were. Our bodies swayed, and I felt the seat of my panties getting wet as he sucked my neck. "Let's get these off," he said huskily, pulling my crop top over my head before kissing down my back until he reached the waistband of my gray leggings. Inching them over my hips, he paid special attention to my ass cheeks, gliding his tongue across my skin and then down to the backs of my thighs.

"Oooh!" He forced me onto my stomach and pushed my thighs apart, burying his face in my middle. "Hmm, Shai, baby!" I bit into the mattress, reaching back and holding his head as he talked to my pussy, making my body shiver.

"You're so fuckin' sweet, love."

Groaning, Shai held my cheeks further apart and sucked my nub, forcing an unexpected orgasm out of me. He stayed on my clit, though, holding my shaking body still as he continued his assault until I was creaming all over his face once again. As I tried to recover, he slid my bottoms the rest of the way off and flipped me over onto my back. He lifted my legs like he was about to change my diaper, holding them together in one hand, and slid his dick between my lips.

"Baby, fuck me!" I whined, growing frustrated from the teasing.

He grinned down at me cockily. "You ready for this dick, love?" He barely had the question out of his mouth before I was nodding furiously. I wanted him in the worst way, and I squirmed beneath him in anticipation.

"Yessss!"

His face turned serious as he finally buried himself inside me, filling me to the hilt. He put his weight into it, stroking me slowly in an upward motion that had me howling his name. Then, just when I was on the verge of cumming, he stopped and sucked on my pussy with my legs still raised high above his head. My soul left my body, and I felt like I was levitating when he slammed into me again, licking the arch of my foot and then sucking my toes.

"Can I put this baby in you, love?" he asked just as tingles shot through my body and had me feeling hot all over. Clearly, he knew exactly what he was doing and was going hard as fuck for another baby, but I was too far gone to deny him.

"Oh, shit, Shai! Fuck yes! I want another baaaby!" I shouted so loud I was positive the neighbors heard me, even though they were half a block away. "I'm bouta cum, baby!"

"Oh, yeah? Wet me up and pull this nut out, Zuri. God damn!" As if I needed permission, my orgasm came at that moment, making my head spin. A second later, he was filling me up, dick pumping as he invaded my uterus.

"Shaaai!" I closed my eyes as my heart pounded in my ears.

He took his time letting my legs down and laughed as he placed wet kisses all over my chest, probably unable to move his damn self.

"Don't Shai me. You said that with yo' whole chest, baby. That's a verbal contract."

"Boy, move!" I cracked up, slapping his back since he was still on top of me. He climbed to his feet and then helped me to stand, still thinking that shit was funny. Even laughing, he was trying to feel me up, but he'd already wasted enough of my time, and I wasn't about to miss a visit with my baby. I tried to walk off and damn near fell, making him laugh harder as he held me up. "Look what you did! It's not funny!" I pouted, mad that I couldn't use my legs like a normal person.

"You right, love. It's not funny." He tried hard to hide his grin. "Come on. I'll help you, and when you finish, yo' shit will probably work like new," His ass said, choking on a laugh, and I gave him a nasty look. "Okay, okay, come on, love." He helped me into the bathroom, leaning me against the counter like I was a damn mannequin while he went to start the water for my shower.

It didn't take long for us both to get cleaned up and handle our oral hygiene. We were at the hospital a couple of hours later. SJ woke up as soon as he heard my voice, dark gray eyes wide, and he was already looking for my nipple when I picked him up.

"Hey, man, were you waiting for me?" I gushed, pinching his little chin before sliding my eyes to Shai. "You can blame yo' daddy for that."

"I'm tryna help him out. He'll understand in a few years." His ass smirked, making all the nurses giggle because they knew exactly what we were talking about.

I rolled my eyes back down to my baby. Turning my back to him, I sat down and covered up so I could feed him and relieve the sudden pressure in my breasts.

As usual, his appetite was hefty. Once he was full, I put him over my shoulder, and he burped before I could even pat his back. I got another two out of him before straightening out my shirt and holding him to my chest. I already knew my baby was going to be spoiled between the way I stayed with him in my arms and when he wasn't, it was because he was in his father's, someone in our family, or the nurses.

"Ms. Miller?" I lifted my head to find Dr. Grimes standing over me, and I gave her a warm smile. She'd been Shai's pediatrician and had taken good care of him since he was born.

"Hey."

"Hey, I just wanted to let you know our little star is ready to be discharged! He's hit every milestone and passed his tests, so I just need to monitor him overnight, and he'll be ready to go in the morning." She smiled, and my eyes instantly watered.

"Really!" I shouted so loud I scared baby Shai, and he jumped, stretching his arms out with a pout. "Ohhh, I'm sorry, baby. But really?" I held him against my chest and asked in a much lower tone, making her nod frantically.

"Yes, really! Congratulations! He'll certainly be missed around here. Don't be surprised if the girls try to stall," she joked, and we shared a laugh before she ran off to handle another patient.

"Shai, baby, they said he can come home tomorrow!" I made sure to keep my voice down, even though I could barely contain myself.

"I heard, love. You think we ready for lil' man full-time?" He couldn't even keep the smile off his face as I mugged him for insinuating that we weren't.

"I know I'm ready, and yo' ass better be ready too, 'cause my baby comin' home tomorrow!" I sang, snapping my fingers and hitting a little two-step that had Shai shaking his head at me. I didn't even care, though. I was so excited. Everything was ready for him, and in less than twenty-four hours, our family would be complete.

SHAI

It was a big day for Zuri and me. Not only were we bringing little man home, but I had a surprise for her ass too. I came down the stairs with Shai's car seat in one hand and his diaper bag in the other. A second later, Zuri and Sevyn came running behind me, but I didn't slow down as they tried to catch up with me. Ever since the police department dropped the charges against her because of Detective Hill's misconduct, she had been at our house more than her ass had been at Zaakir's, and they stayed trying to double-team me.

"Shai, wait! We can't leave without picking his outfit!" Zuri was the first to catch up, and she held two outfits up to me to pick from while Sevyn came around with two of her own.

"No, pick one of these!"

"He gon' fuck around and come home in a onesie if y'all don't figure that shit out in the next five seconds," I said once I made it to the garage door.

They'd been arguing for the last hour over what outfit they wanted him to wear, and I was already over it. The warning had them both scrambling away from me to ask Zaakir, who would care more about that shit than me. With them out of my face, I was able to strap in his seat and head back inside to see if they were finally ready. When I made it to the living room, they had managed to narrow the selections down to two, and Zaakir's crazy ass was pacing in front of them, stroking his chin like he was in deep thought.

"This a hard one," he mused, looking back and forth between them.

"Man, this one is fine!" I quickly snatched the hanger that Zuri was holding and then the one from Sevyn. "And this can be a spare. That's what we going with. If not, I'll just go get him by myself, and y'all gon' miss being able to take pictures."

Zuri clapped gleefully while Sevyn sat pouting, but at that point, I was just ready to get him home after all these months.

"You're a hater, bro!" Zaakir yelled at my back as I carried the outfits with me to the car, but they all followed since they knew I wasn't playing about leaving them.

I held Zuri's door open for her, and she gave me a kiss as she hopped inside, still celebrating her win. After handing her the clothes, I shut her door and went around to my side while Zaakir and Sevyn hopped in their car.

"You scared?" I asked once we'd been on the road for a while, and I felt her hand trembling in mine.

She looked gorgeous in a bright pink sundress that tied around the neck and cinched just under her breasts, making her cleavage look extra juicy. Her hair was in a high bun with two curled pieces hanging on either side of her face. I couldn't stop looking at her and feeling lucky that she was mine.

Tilting her head, she fluttered her lashes at me. "Not really, just a little nervous... You?"

"Naw, I think we got this." I didn't even have to think about it. I was excited as hell.

Shai was just starting to stay awake for longer periods of time, so I was looking forward to hanging out with him. I'd already made preparations for the time I'd be off, and although I would still be available if it was an emergency, I was hoping I wouldn't have to leave him to go in.

"Ooooh, you're so sexy when you're in daddy mode." She shuddered, giving me that look, and I had to adjust my dick.

"You better quit playin'. I'll pull this bitch over, and you got on a dress! Shai gon' have a little sister sooner if you keep tryna entice me, love." Her cheeks flushed, and she pressed her thighs together.

"Damn, are we gonna be those parents?" She laughed after a minute, burying her face in her hands, and I raised a brow.

"Care to elaborate?"

"We're gonna be *those* parents." She reiterated, like that would help me to know what type of parents she was talking about. "Oh gosh, Shai! You know, the type of parents that's always embarrassing their kids being mannish."

I eyed her for a second before bursting out laughing because we were definitely going to be that. I quickly agreed.

"Yeah, I can see that, but at least they'll know what it's like to have parents who actually love each other and show affection." I shrugged. "You should be happy, though. Our kids won't be addicted to that toxic shit like my cousin and yo' best friend." It was a joke, but Zuri's neck snapped, immediately offended for her girl when all I was trying to do was make her feel good.

"Don't come for my bestie. They've been doing good lately, and you know it."

"You're right, love." I decided to agree just to avoid ruining our vibe.

The truth was, Zaakir and Sevyn were crazy as hell apart, but their asses were even crazier together. That shit worked for them, though, and despite the shit they always had going on, I had to admit they made each other better.

"Good answer." Zuri laughed, but I already knew that.

We made it to the hospital a short time later, where my parents and her mama were waiting. Zuri's indecisive ass changed her mind and decided to go with Sevyn's outfit, which was a white Gucci Romper with a red and green stripe across the chest and a matching hat with the Gucci print. His feet were still too small for shoes, so he only had a pair of socks. While Zuri was distracted with dressing him, I prepared for her surprise that everybody was in on, even the nurses on the unit. They'd made a lot of exceptions for me to be able to do it there, and I wanted everything to go off without a hitch. Sevyn helped keep her busy, taking a ton of pictures of her and the baby.

Once everything was all set, I crept up behind her as Sevyn turned on her Beats Pill, and "Someone" by Musiq Soulchild began playing quietly. Zuri turned around with her brows raised in confusion, but when she saw me down on one knee with our families behind me, her crybaby ass started tearing up.

"Zuri Miller, since the day we met, there was something about you that had me doing shit I've never done. I saw a future with you before I even knew that it was possible, and just when I thought I'd lost you forever, God came through and blessed us with our son. Out of all the women in this world, I know *you're* my someone, and all I want to do is spend the rest of my life giving you everything you deserve plus more. Would you do me the greatest honor and be my wife, love?"

The whole time I'd been planning and getting ready, I was calm, cool, and collected, but now that I was in front of her and on my knees awaiting her answer, I was nervous as fuck. I let out a sigh of relief when she finally nodded and stuck out a shaky hand to me. Besides seeing Shai take his first breath, this moment had to be the best of my life. I slid Zuri's five-carat, pear shaped diamond ring on her finger and pulled her into a hug as everyone in the room clapped.

"I can't believe you did this, baby! I love you so much!"

"I love you too," I told her, wiping the few tears that had managed to slip out. I didn't think I'd ever seen her so beautiful, and I couldn't wait to marry her ass.

SEVYN

I listened to Zaakir talk shit through my AirPods as I stood in line at my favorite café. He was mad I hadn't given him a quickie before leaving for work that morning, even though he knew there was no such thing as a quickie with him. Now, he was on my phone talking shit because I'd snuck out on him, and the shit was hilarious.

"You laughing?" he asked, unable to hide his attitude.

I swallowed the laugh trying to escape as I moved with the line.

"No, bae, but yo' thirsty self can wait until I get off. You act like you don't have nothin' better to do than lay up in it." I tried to lower my voice because this was not 8 a.m. café talk, and I didn't want anybody in my business. The girl in the line next to me raised her brow, and I turned my back to her.

"Shiiit, I don't," he came back quickly, and I rolled my eyes at how serious he sounded. "I told yo' ass I could stay in that mutha-fucka! I wasn't playing, girl, shit!"

"I'm not bouta play with you, Zaakir." I huffed, making it to the counter and putting his ass on mute until I finished putting in our order while he talked his shit in my ear.

"Shit, I wish you would play with this muhfucka. He definitely callin' you!" He cackled, and I quickly unmuted him. "Shut up, Zaakir!" He had me blushing as I grabbed the tray and made my way outside. It was super warm, and I hated that I could already feel sweat on my back as soon as I stepped out the door.

"I'm just saying," he mumbled while I took a sip of my iced coffee and moaned. It tasted so good, which was why I was willing to drive so far out and stand in the long ass lines. Shit, I considered keeping Tyrese's drink. It was that good. "See, you playin'. Fuck you doin' all that for? I'm bouta hang up on yo' ass!"

Laughing, I prepared to cross the street to my truck. "You're the one who called me, and I been tryna get you off the phone!" I watched for a chance to rush across the street, and when I didn't see any cars, I switched across, tucking my phone against my shoulder so I could unlock the doors. There was so much going on, and with the added distraction of Zaakir's voice, I didn't hear the car approaching until it was almost too late. A black Benz sped past, and I had to press my body against my truck just to avoid getting hit. It was so close I could feel the heat off it, and my heart pounded.

"Sevyn! Sevyn, you okay?" Zaakir was shouting in my ear, but I couldn't answer him or the multiple people who had witnessed it and were asking if I was okay. Panting, I jumped in my truck and pressed my head against the steering wheel as I tried to get my breathing and heart rate under control. I felt like I was going to be sick. "Sevyn, say something. Baby, are you okay?"

It took me a few seconds to be able to speak. I swallowed the lump in my throat and finally nodded like he could see me.

"Y-yeah, I'm fine," I stammered.

I couldn't believe I'd almost gotten hit by a damn car. It was a pretty busy intersection, so I knew there was wild driving, but it didn't feel random to me. I wracked my brain, trying to think of a description outside of it being a black Benz.

"You didn't just scream like you were fine, and you damn sure don't sound like you are right now. What's your location? I'll come get you," he offered, but I quickly declined.

I'd finally gotten my life back, no police, no case, and most importantly, no Tramel. I absolutely wasn't going to go running every time something happened. Shaking my head, I started my car.

"No, I'm fine, bae. You know how these muthafuckas drive out here," I dismissed, taking my time as I pulled out of my parking space.

Zaakir didn't sound convinced, but he also didn't want to put too much into it. He talked to me the rest of the way to my shop, and I was eventually able to calm down. I convinced myself I was tweaking after having so much shit happen in such a short amount of time. Maybe I was just being paranoid.

Thankfully, the rest of the day went off without any issues. Once we closed the shop, and Tyrese suggested a drink, I was down for it. There was a bar not too far from the shop, so we all drove down. We could hear the music before we even got out of our cars. It wasn't packed, though, allowing us enough room to move around and easily find a spot at the bar.

"What you gettin'?" Tyrese quizzed as he snapped his fingers to the old Avant that was playing. He knew about what had happened that morning and had been doing his best to keep my mind off it. I had to say it was certainly working, and I knew a couple drinks would help, too.

"I want Patron shots," I quickly said, already knowing that I'd be good after a couple and could go home and have Zaakir fuck the memory of that morning away.

"Oooh, you bouta get that Patron dick, ain't you? I see you, boss lady!" Niqua's ass called me out, and we all cracked up.

"And is!"

"See, that's why I gotta stop hanging with y'all tied down bitches. Y'all gon' get a couple drinks in you, then rush home! I'm out all night!" Raven said, waving us off, and I shrugged.

"Sure am! I love my man!" I slapped hands with Tyrese as the bartender finally came over to get our orders.

"Sis just mad she ain't got a man," he said, only loud enough for me to hear, but I already knew that.

We quickly got our orders in, and by the time I finished my second shot and danced to a few songs, I was ready to go. I used to talk shit about the 'my man, my man' girls, but now I completely understood what they were talking about because all I wanted to do was go home to my man. That was easier said than done, though, because Tyrese and the girls were not trying to let me leave. They talked shit until I stayed for another couple of rounds, and by the time we downed those, I was ready to go home to my man.

"Okay, I'm going home. Y'all done kept me out long enough," I finally said after polishing off the fruity drink Niqua had ordered us.

"Awww, party pooper!"

"Lame!"

"Don't go yet!"

A chorus of complaints filled the bar since we'd been the life of the party, but I'd long since reached my limit, and I probably wouldn't even be able to drive home in my current state. I slid off my barstool and threw my hands up to quiet them down and was met with groans.

"I don't wanna leave, but I gotta go right nowwwww!" I sang, making them all laugh like I'd said the funniest shit in the world. "Naw, for real, y'all, I'ma see you ladies in the morning, and don't think I'm cutting y'all any slack just cause y'all got drunk tonight!" I squinted at Raven in particular because she was known to be late because of partying the night before.

"Damn, why you gotta look at me?" she grumbled with a pout.

"I got these fools. Let me walk you out, though. I don't want you outside alone this time of night." Tyrese climbed to his feet and tried to shake off the effects of the many shots he'd taken as I searched my purse for my keys. As soon as I fished them out, they slipped from my fingers, and I rushed and tried to catch them, damn near falling on my head. "Damn, girl, you tryna get a concussion?" He managed to catch me with a huff.

"Shit, my bad. I just got a little dizzy. I'm good now," I asserted, standing upright.

"Yeah, ayite, you won't be needing these." Tyrese plucked my keys out of my hand before I could react and shoved them into the pocket of his jeans. While I knew I was tipsy before, I really knew I was when the thought of how he looked getting out of skinny jeans entered my mind.

"What? I'm good." I frowned, reaching to snatch them back, and almost fell again, making my purse slip from my shoulder.

Sucking his teeth, Tyrese picked that up, too, and slipped it on his arm.

"See, yo' ass absolutely ain't good, and you not about to have Zaaaaaakiiiir tryna shoot me for letting his precious woman drive home this tore up. I'm getting you a Lyft, girl, and we can just come back for your car tomorrow." Tyrese already had his phone out, typing away before I could object. Although I didn't want to ride with anybody else, I went ahead and agreed. "I'll be right back, y'all!" he told the girls as I called my baby to tell him I was on the way.

"Aye, baby, where you at?" It seemed like Zaakir answered on the first ring, and the concern in his voice had my stomach full of butterflies.

"I'm leaving now. Tyrese and 'nem were holding me hostage, bae, but I'm waiting for my Lyft," I whined, shooting his ass an evil look.

"Fuck you ridin' in that shit for when you got a man with multiple cars? I'll come get you, Sev." I could already hear him moving around, probably finding clothes to put on, and I simpered despite myself.

"Noooo, you know they charge when you cancel, and he already got one for me. Besides, I want you ass naked when I get there, so I can just jump on it as soon as I come in the door." I moaned lowly, biting my lip as my clit jumped just thinking about the good ass dick he was about to give me.

"Broooo, you drunk as fuck for real! Don't be sayin' no shit like ass naked to me, girl!" He tried to chastise me, but I could hear the amusement in his voice.

"Why not? I'm tryna put this WAP on you."

"Aye, Sev, tell Tyrese I'm gon' fuck him up for letting you get so drunk, man."

"Nah uh, Zaaaaakiiiir, don't be tryna come for me! It was Niqua ass feeding her all those Hot Pussies!" Tyrese quickly spoke up, shaking his head.

"Hot what? What the hell y'all asses had going on?" Zaakir snapped, and I fell into a fit of giggles as he went off.

"Bae! Bae!" I called, trying to get his attention since he was still fussing as a car pulled up in front of us. "Don't be surprised, baby, it's just me. Don't be surprised, boy, when I bust it wide! I hypnotize you with this pussy. Now you feel like you can fly!" I sang, winding like he could see me.

"Girl, get yo' freaky ass in the car!" Tyrese sucked his teeth, opening the back door for me once he double-checked the driver. I danced over at him, grinning, and gave him air kisses as I slipped into the backseat.

"Yeah, I'm fuckin' that nigga up! Yo' ass too drunk," Zaakir said, making me laugh as the driver took off.

"Not too drunk to hop on that dick, tho!" I whispered loudly.

"Man, how long it's bouta take you to get here?" he wanted to know.

I looked out the window to see where we were. I could tell we were still in the same area as my shop, so I figured a few minutes away, which meant it'd probably be another half hour to forty-five minutes before I reached him at his house. We spent a few days out of the week at his house and the rest at mine, but it was beginning to be a lot of running back and forth. I'd already considered us just moving in together at that point because we were together so much; I just hadn't been brave enough to mention it to him. We'd only just gotten back right, and I wasn't trying to rock the boat by forcing my way into his space.

"Umm, it'll probably be another half hour or so," I told him, frowning when I felt the driver slow to a stop. "Excuse me, this isn't where I'm going." I rolled my eyes. I was going to fuck Tyrese up if he got the wrong address with his drunk ass. This was exactly why I wanted to drive myself or, at the very least, order my own car. "Helloooo!" I leaned forward, dropping the phone from my ear when his ass acted like he couldn't hear me. My drunkenness had me in a state that I wasn't immediately alarmed, only irritated. I could still faintly hear Zaakir's voice as I tried again. "Sir, I'm not going here."

My words got stuck in my throat when Rome turned around, grinning sinisterly with a gun in my face. "I know, sis. You comin' with me."

"Rome, I—"

"SHUT THE FUCK UP! I swear I always told bro you talked too fuckin' much! Give me that damn phone! Now!" he shouted, and I shakily handed it over.

My mind raced as I tried to figure a way out of this situation. I felt around for my purse and cursed myself when I realized I'd been so busy fucking around on the phone that I'd left it with Tyrese.

Rome put the phone on speaker, laughing as Zaakir called him everything but a child of God and threatened his family. "That ain't the way to talk to the nigga that got yo' girl, boy!"

"Nigga, I will kill you!" Zaakir seethed.

I blinked back tears as I tried the door and realized his ass had the child safety lock on, and the same with the windows.

"No! I'll kill her, so you better do what the fuck I say 'cause I ain't got shit to lose! Now, I'm gon' call you in a little bit with some instructions. I'd advise you to answer and not try any funny shit, or this hoe gon' lose her life!" He hung up while Zaakir was still talking and tossed my phone out the window before turning his murderous gaze my way. It was clear he meant everything he said, and this was no longer the nigga I considered a brother for years.

"Rome, you don't have to do this—" I hiccupped, losing the battle with my tears as they poured down my face.

Instead of responding, he drew back, smacking me across the face with the gun so hard I saw stars before everything went black.

ZAAKIR

The next day, I was still waiting on a call from Rome's goofy ass. When a half hour had gone by without any word from him, I'd called my cousin and Pops, trying to get a location on that nigga. She'd tracked Sevyn's phone to the front of an apartment building, and we found it just lying in the street with a cracked screen. In my heart, I knew his ass wasn't stupid enough to have left it where he was hiding her, but that didn't stop me from knocking on doors. I didn't give a fuck that it was two in the morning. Everyone in that building was going to get up.

Shit, I even checked the basement, and when I came up empty, I prepared to go door to door, but Shai and Casa forced my black ass back in the car. They didn't think Rome would've left the phone right where he was, and they felt like we were wasting time over there. They tried to advise me to go home and wait for the nigga to call, but instead, I headed up to the bar, hoping Tyrese and the other hoes Sevyn had been with were still there living it up while my girl was snatched up. Two out of the three were there at the bar, probably in the same spot she'd left them in. I lowkey started to knock Tyrese the fuck out as soon as I laid eyes on them and saw Sevyn's purse on the seat next to him, but the fact that the Niqua bitch was gone and had supposedly left right after Sevyn had me rushing to pick her up.

With three niggas pointing guns in their faces, Raven and Tyrese were more than willing to get in the truck with Shai and me while my pops followed us. "What's this bitch address?" I asked no one in particular as I pulled out of the lot.

"She stays right off Halsted on 87th and Emerald," Tyrese was quick to say, and I sped in that direction.

It seemed funny as hell to me that she decided to leave right after Sevyn, so she was suspect number one in my book. Unfortunately, my girl wasn't there, but I snatched her ass up anyway.

Now, a total of eight hours had gone by, and none of them had anything to say as they sat on Sevyn's couch, watching me. I'd been questioning them like I was the fucking police, wanting to know what they did and where all they'd gone, but wasn't shit popping up. I even had Tyrese's bitch ass show me the Lyft app on his phone just to confirm there actually was one because I was suspicious of all their asses. Sevyn went out with me and Zuri often and hadn't shit like this happened before, but the minute she stays out late with them, she gets kidnapped.

"This is fucking crazy." Zuri sighed as she bounced baby Shai on her shoulder. "I can't believe Rome would do some shit like this to her after everything Tramel put her through! If he hurts her, I swear to God!" She fought back tears, and Shai pulled her into a hug.

"I'll break every bone in that nigga's body!" I sneered with one fist balled since I held my gun in the other. Just thinking about Sevyn being hurt by that broke ass, dick riding nigga had me hot.

"We're gonna get Sevyn back, love. Just calm down." Shai sent a look over her head at me, but I wasn't trying to hear shit. His girl was right there with their son, so I didn't give a fuck what he was talking about.

"I'm bouta go round up that nigga's team. Fuck it." I

shrugged, heading toward the door. "Y'all keep an eye on these muthafuckas. Ain't nobody leavin' this bitch 'til my girl back."

"Shai, go with him and make sure he doesn't do nothin' crazy." I could hear Zuri pleading with his ass, but there wasn't going to be much his ass could do to stop me with the way I was feeling.

I really wanted to burn the whole fucking city down. Of course, his babysitting ass did what she wanted and followed me out, but not before I repeated the orders to Casa. It was probably better that he be the one to stay anyway because Shai would've fucked around and let one of them hoes leave if they laid it on thick enough and if Zuri was in his ear.

I popped the trunk on my Hellcat and pulled out the AK that was resting back there while Shai looked at me in disapproval. I was trying to do damage; I didn't give a fuck what he was talking about. Hopping behind the steering wheel, I laid the assault rifle across my lap as Shai climbed into the passenger side. I drove out to the spots Elle had been able to find back when she found out all of Sevyn's dirt, but as soon as I reached the first block, I saw that the house there was deserted. The same went for the next four houses, and suddenly, it all made sense why Rome's ass had snatched Sevyn up. He was obviously desperate for cash.

Pissed, I sat in front of the last house, trying to control the rage I felt brewing. "Aye, cuz, you gone have to chill, man. That nigga tryna get money. He a street nigga, so he knows without Sevyn, he don't have shit to bargain with. Trust me, that nigga gon' call. Let's just head back to the house so we can strategize when he does."

Just like Zuri said, his ass was trying to be the voice of reason because I was about to burn the house to the ground. I didn't give a damn that them niggas were gone and even less of a damn about the others on the block.

"On my soul, if he touches her, bro."

"Don't worry, muthafuckas. I'm gon' make sure that nigga get his. That's my wife's best friend, and yo' woman, ain't no way we letting this ride. Sevyn's family," he stressed, holding out his fist.

I dapped him up quick before pulling off and heading back to the crib to await his call.

"You think he working with either of them hoes in there?" I quizzed as we pulled back into Sevyn's driveway. I looked up at the house like I could see through the walls or some shit, and he shrugged.

"I don't know. I wouldn't put shit past anybody these days, but if I had to guess, I'd say no. They been up in this bitch for hours. Somebody would've messaged ol' boy for him to call so we could get this shit over with."

I kept my eyes on the house as I nodded because that made sense. Since this was about the money, somebody as desperate as Rome would've called, and his partner in crime would've been making sure he did.

"Right, right," I agreed absentmindedly, but the feel of my phone vibrating had me rushing to answer.

My heart pounded when my phone rang, and a random number flashed across my screen. I held it up for Shai to see before answering with him on speaker.

"Damn, thirsty ass nigga. You answering on the first ring like you my bitch!" His lame ass cackled like that shit was funny.

"Man, did you call to get this money or play on the phone, bitch ass nigga?" my face balled up, and Shai shot me a look, but I was tired of his ass, and he hadn't even called but twice.

"You mad?" Rome continued to laugh, and I gripped the phone tightly. "Ayite, I'ma stop fuckin' with you. If you want yo' girl back, I'm gon' need you to come up with a half mil, and don't try to say you ain't got it or that it's gon' take some time 'cause I know y'all A'santi niggas holdin', and if you ain't, yo' daddy damn sure is! Shit, yo' cousin's pops got that bag too! This really a steal if you think about it, but I guess that depends on how much you love this bitch. Tramel was willin' to sell everybody out and die behind that pussy. What you willin' to do for it?" His sick ass laughed, knowing there wasn't much I could say since he held all the cards.

I damn sure wasn't about to confirm for his ass, but I could vouch that the pussy was worth way more than the little shit he was asking for. Gritting my teeth, I kept the insults that were on the tip of my tongue back and managed to say, "Okay, half a mil, but I want confirmation of life, bitch." I couldn't stop that shit from coming out.

"I got yo' bitch, literally, but I'll let that shit slide."

I heard movement in the background, like he'd covered the phone before he came back on the line. "Aye, bitch, say hey to yo' nigga!" he demanded.

"Zaakir, baby, don't give this nigga shit!"

"Sev!" I released a breath I didn't even know I was holding when I heard Sevyn's stubborn ass yelling. She was going to be a hood bitch even if it killed her. If this wasn't such a serious situation, I would've laughed at her trying to act hard. "I'm comin' to get you, bae!"

"That's enough! Ol' Liam Neeson ass nigga!" Rome came back on the line. "You got 'til seven p.m. to call and say you got that money! Any longer, and I'm gon' be wearin' this bitch brains!" he said before the line went dead.

I was already calculating our funds in my mind as I climbed out of the car with Shai hot on my heels. That nigga Rome was right, we definitely had the money, but I didn't know if it was all liquid. For sure, I had about two hundred thousand in cash stashed, but I'd need to dip into other reserves for the rest, even though I didn't intend for that nigga to ever get to spend it.

"You know I got you with whatever you need, cuz," Shai said as we headed inside.

I hadn't even noticed extra cars in the driveway, but Zuri's mama, Queen, and Gio were all in attendance now.

"We got the call. He wants half a mil by seven," I said to no one in particular, and immediately, the Raven bitch gasped. All of Sevyn's stylists looked out of place and uncomfortable in a room full of criminals and surrounded by guns. I didn't have any use for them since I'd gotten in contact with Rome, so I pointed in their direction and nodded toward the door. "Aye, y'all, get the fuck up outta here."

"But what about Sevyn?" Tyrese stood up slowly but didn't move while the other two damn near ran.

"I'm gon' get her." I shrugged because, at that point, it should've been common sense.

Nodding, he slid past us, and I had to resist the urge to knock his ass the fuck out, but I knew Sevyn would've been pissed. Once I heard the door close behind them, I nodded at Shai, who immediately went to get Elle on the phone. I wanted eyes and ears on them hoes, just in case they actually knew more than they were letting on. I was going to have her hack their phones, and if they went anywhere suspect, I was gonna be on their asses.

"Will we be able to come up with that so soon? I know I'm not rich, but I have maybe ten thousand," Zuri offered, but I instantly shook my head. I'd never take her money, especially when she'd just had my baby cousin.

"Yeah, I got it, Zuri. Thanks, though."

"Zaakir, I know I haven't always approved of your relationship with Sevyn, but it's obvious you love her, and who the fuck am I to stand in the way of that? Yo' mama would be proud, son," Casa said, putting a hand on my shoulder, which was probably the closest he'd come to hugging my ass. "I got two hundred thousand stashed from my trick fund." He tried to hide behind a cough, and Ms. Zora cleared her throat, making him add, "I don't need it no more, damn! That's why I'm tryna give it to his ass!" he pleaded, shocking everyone as he moved to her side.

"Ma! I know you fuckin' lyin'!" Zuri gasped, wide eyed.

"Girl, don't ma me!" Ms. Zora waved her off, deading the conversation.

I shared a look with Queen, and she shrugged like she wasn't aware, but there was no telling with her ass since she'd kept her and Gio's shit a secret.

"Well, you know, whatever you need, I can assist," Gio said next. "Men, weapons, money."

Nodding, I contemplated how much help we'd need, happy for the distraction since this shit had turned into a Maury episode. We didn't need weapons since we had an arsenal of our own, but I wasn't too sure about his racist ass men.

"I'm gon' let you know," I told him just as Shai's ass came from the back and gave me a head nod to let me know it was done.

Now, all I had to do was get the money and guns together, then go get my girl.

SEVYN

I watched Rome go from pacing to sitting to pacing again and wondered if his ass was on drugs. He had to have been to try it with Zaakir without any type of backup, but I guess that was better for me. Despite what I'd said, I knew Zaakir was coming for me, and I also knew that Rome was going to die behind this shit. I certainly couldn't wait to see his ass die. I wanted front row seats. Better yet, I wanted parts of it.

"Stop fuckin' lookin' at me!" he screamed, and I nodded inwardly. *Yeah, this nigga cracked out!*

I silently rolled my eyes and looked away. There wasn't much to see in the crappy old warehouse he was holding me in. It was dark, smelly, and wet with mushy piles of cardboard and random ass tables. I wondered what the fuck was in there before. The stench alone made me feel like I had to throw up every time my stomach growled since I hadn't eaten. Shit, I hadn't moved from that spot since he brought me there, meaning, in addition to my stomach aching for food, my bladder was on ten after all the liquor I'd had. It was getting to the point that I felt like if I moved a certain way, I'd be sitting in a puddle.

"Can I go to the bathroom?" I forced myself to ask as nicely as possible, even though I was sure my face showed how much it pained me to do so.

"No, piss on yourself, bitch!" he spat, not even stopping his stride. "Why the fuck this muthafucka not answering?"

My brows shot up at that because, for one, I didn't know he was calling anybody, and for two, I knew he was waiting for Zaakir's call, so I was confused about who he was trying to get on the phone. In my heart, I knew Tramel was dead, but I couldn't help being a little afraid that he'd bring his dead ass around the corner at any minute. That would be the last thing I needed because, at least with just Rome, I knew the money could sway him. If Tramel was alive, he'd be dead set on revenge, and my ass would be in the ground.

I squeezed my legs together as that thought alone had my muscles feeling weaker before they just completely gave up. Hot ass piss that seemed to last forever soaked my jeans, and I dropped my head in shame because even though it was nasty as hell, I was completely relieved.

"Daaaaamn, you really pissed on yourself! Not the real-life Tasha St. Patrick!" he teased. "I never would've thought I'd see the day."

"I should've pissed on you, bum ass nigga! Up in here kidnapping just to get by! Aww, yo' big daddy Tramel is dead, so you're out here alone and defenseless." I poked out my lip mockingly.

Before I knew what hit me, he'd crossed the small space between us and punched me in the mouth so hard I just knew I was going to be spitting out teeth. Blood filled my mouth as my head whipped back around, and I spit it on his dingy Jordans, even though it hurt to even do so. "You gon' have to hit harder than that if you goin' up against my nigga—"

The words were barely out when he hit me again, this time making me too woozy to talk shit. "Yeah, I told you to shut up, bitch! All this shit is yo' fault! Business was good! Money was good! Tramel even let you have niggas on the side, but then you had to go and try to leave him for one! You see this warehouse?

Just four months ago, it was full of product and money, but when yo' stupid ass pulled that shit and made that nigga lose his mind, he sold us out to sell you out! I ain't never met no street nigga that would do some shit like that! I swear you gotta have platinum pussy for niggas to lose their fuckin' minds behind you like they doin'! I was tempted to find out, but not with you smellin' like you're sittin' in piss," he cracked. "Oh wait, you are!" His crazy ass stopped laughing long enough to punch me again, making the room grow black.

"Hmmm," I moaned, trying to open my eyes and grab my throbbing head, but I couldn't do either.

That's when I remembered that Rome had me tied to a chair and was just punching me in the face like I was a fucking man. I tried unsuccessfully to at least hold my head up, and when I couldn't, silent tears rolled down my face, stinging my skin. Since I couldn't see, I listened to see if Rome was close by, and I vaguely made out whispering.

"What the fuck, Rome! You said she wouldn't be hurt! Why the fuck she over there looking like she got in the ring with Apollo Creed?" I perked up, hearing someone else speaking. Obviously, it was his partner in crime, so it wasn't any help, but at least I knew it wasn't Tramel.

"That bitch was running her mouth! If you don't wanna look like that, too, you better stop worrying about her and tell me if that nigga had the money!"

My heart pounded, hoping that whoever it was said that they'd gotten the money from Zaakir so I could be let go. I didn't know how much time had passed, but my pee was now cold and itching my skin, in addition to the fact that my face felt like a heavy ass empty balloon.

"I don't know. He just said how much you wanted, but judging from the people in the room, they can definitely get it. Hell, he probably had it in the house right then."

My head instantly tilted at that. If this person had been around Zaakir and his family, then that meant they knew me, which meant there was a snake in my circle. It didn't take but a few seconds for it to register who would've been that close to Zaakir since I only had a handful of people I kept around, and I couldn't help but cry.

"Really, Tyrese? You really let this nigga do this to me?" My voice cracked, and the room grew silent before I heard them whispering harshly but much more quiet this time. "Bitch, I know it's you. Ain't no point in hiding!"

"I'm sorry, Sevyn! Damn! I was just trying to help a friend. All he wants is the money, and then we were going to leave and—"

"And you thought you were gonna be able to look me in my face after what this nigga did to me?" I asked humorlessly. "I'm sittin' in fuckin' piss with my face mangled, and you thought it was gon' be okay? Is this the nigga you been fuckin'?" I just had to know because outside of dick, I couldn't see why Tyrese would want to help Rome when they normally couldn't stand each other, which now seemed like an act to throw me off.

"Bitch, ain't no nigga fuckin' me!" Rome was quick to correct me, and if my feelings weren't so hurt, I would've laughed. It was just like a nigga to try to make the gay shit he was on less gay.

"Really, Rome?"

"You a dirty muthafucka, Tyrese, and I hope Zaakir kills yo' ass!" I never thought I'd say some shit like that to a friend, but for him to play me after everything I'd done for him was crazy. I swear this was just a year of revelations because I was quickly learning there were even fewer people I could count on than I thought.

"Why? 'Cause I chose my man this time like you always do! Let's not forget I ended up doin' illegal shit 'cause of you choosing Tramel, and then I got locked up because you decided you wanted to choose Zaakir!" he shouted, and I could barely make out him slapping his chest. "I didn't want you to get hurt because I love you. You're my bitch, but you want me dead, Sevyn? I can't believe you," this delusional ass nigga had the nerve to say, and I laughed bitterly.

"Bitch, fuck you!"

"Fuck me! Fuck you, Sevyn—" The unmistakable sound of a bullet whizzing in the air silenced whatever he was about to say, and blood splashed all over my face.

"Oh, fuck!" Rome cursed as glass broke around us from the multiple bullets flying.

I struggled to get my hands free, and when I couldn't, I rocked from side to side until my chair toppled over. Ducking my head, I screamed in terror until the bullets finally stopped, and everything grew silent. I squeezed my eyes shut and started praying, which was some shit I almost never did.

"SEVYN!"

"*Zaakir!*" I let out a whimper when I heard Zaakir's voice, and heavy footsteps echoed loudly. His scent hit my nose before he reached me and yanked my chair upright.

"What the fuck! What he do to you? I'm gon' kill that nigga!" He touched my face tenderly, and I nuzzled against his hand as more tears slipped out. "Aye, bring that muthafucka to me! I want his ass alive!" He untied me and lifted me in his arms bridal style as people ran to carry out his orders.

As soon as I felt the fresh air outside, I took a deep breath. I was alive and had managed to escape death again, thanks to Zaakir. My grip tightened around his neck as he tried to place me in the car, and he chuckled lowly.

"You not tryna let me go?" he quizzed, tickling my face with his breath, and I held on tighter.

"Nope, never."

ZURI

I held SJ close to my chest and rubbed his back in small circles, eventually getting the burp I was working for. It was so loud he scared himself, and I had to laugh at the way he jumped. Once I was sure he was done, I carried him over to his bed and laid him down before turning on his mobile with the lights. Almost immediately, his eyes began to droop, and I sent a thank you to the man upstairs. He wasn't a crybaby when his daddy was around, but when it was just me, he was attached to the titty something serious and would cry as soon as I tried to detach. I loved my baby, but sometimes, I liked to walk around without a little human attached to me.

"Did you make him go to bed?" Sevyn's voice was loud as hell in my ear.

It had been a little over a month since we'd gotten her back, and I was grateful as hell. So grateful that I made it a habit to talk to her ass every day. Plus, I knew she was in a dark place after finding out that Tyrese was helping Rome. I honestly never would have thought he would do something like that to her, of all people, but dick will make you do some crazy things.

I waited until I shut SJ's door and went to my room before answering. "Sure did. It's his bedtime, Sevyn."

"Who got a bedtime? Do I need to come over there? 'Cause I feel like you're abusing my baby. Where's Shai? I know he's not goin' for no bedtime."

"Shai ain't here, and even if he was, SJ would be his little ass in the bed."

"Baby! Bae! Go start the car so we can get our nephew. Zuri's over there abusing him!" she shouted for Zaakir, and I rolled my eyes. I didn't know what she was calling him for because she was the only one scared of him.

"I'm not bouta play with you, Sevyn. Get that ice pack and lay yo' ass down!" I heard him snap and busted out laughing.

"That's what yo' ass get! You heard the man!" I teased, getting comfortable in my own bed.

It had been an eventful week, and I had been getting sleepier much earlier than normal. I attributed it to baby Shai coming home and keeping me running most days and nights, but I still wouldn't have traded motherhood for anything in the world.

"Girl, Zaakir don't run shit over here but his mouth! Don't let him fool you." I could hear rustling in the background as she sucked her teeth, and I knew her black ass was doing what he'd said, even as she denied it.

"Yeah, okay. Have Casa and my mama been over there yet?" I asked, changing the subject.

It had been a surprise to find out that, of all people, my mama had decided to mess with Zaakir's daddy, and it was an even bigger surprise that he'd switched up his ways. I thought they were cute together, especially the way he spoiled her rotten. She'd really never had it like that before, and it was good to see her get what she deserved.

"Yep! They had Zaakir's crazy ass over here trying to google if it would make you his sister/cousin since you and Shai getting married. You should've seen it. Casa was mad as hell!" We laughed together because I could imagine his grown ass doing some shit like that. "I think they're cute, though."

"Me too, hoe. They've been making their rounds, so they were over here checking on us too, and he was being so sweet, pulling out her chair and whispering in her ear. He even had her old ass blushing, and you know Zora don't be blushing. I just hope he keeps it up 'cause it would be awkward as hell if they ever fell out."

"Girl, it would be one hundred times worse than it was with yo' daddy 'cause they both have crazy tendencies."

I had to lift my phone and make sure I was still talking to the same girl who argued with Zaakir's ass every chance she got before snorting. "The nerve."

"The nerve who, hoe?"

"The nerve of you! Y'all be over there acting a damn fool, so I know you're not talking," I called her out, making her laugh.

"Yeah, me and bae be going at it, but that's my boo, though."

"Awwww!" The way her voice softened was so cute. I loved that she was in love and that Zaakir didn't play about her. They fussed and fought, but Stevie Wonder could see that they were made for each other.

"See, you doin' too much now!" She tried to play it off, but I could hear the smile in her voice.

"Girl, stop. We bouta be rocking matching rings and matching baby seats. Matter fact, I'm wishing twins on you since you wanna play!"

"Ooooh, I wish the fuck his ass would knock me up with two babies! On my nonexistent mama, I'm gon' give him hell!" she hollered, and I fell out laughing.

"Not nonexistent!"

"Whoever her ass is. Shit, you got me ready to go in there and slap his ass, and I ain't even pregnant!" She was on a roll, and my stomach was hurting from laughing so hard.

"Who the fuck you gon' slap!" Zaakir could be heard in the background, and I knew I'd started some shit.

"You, nigga! Put some twins in here if you want to!"

"What the fuck yo' silly ass talkin' 'bout! The way you be tellin' me to shoot yo' shit up every night, you 'bout got quintuplets growin' in there!"

"That'll be the first time a person ever grew wings and flew away. 'Cause if I push five babies out at one time, you gon' be a single daddy!"

"Shiiiit, the hoes love single daddies! Don't let me tell 'em they all got different mamas. They gon' be on my nuts for real!"

"Don't fuckin' play with me, Zaakir!"

"Now yo' ass mad. That's what you get!"

"Yeah, you did say you were gon' leave, sis." I shrugged, and she sucked her teeth.

"Whose side you on? Traitor ass hoe!" she quipped, making me shake my head.

Listening to them go at it would make the sanest person go crazy.

"I'm bouta be on the hanging up side," I said just as the alarm system alerted me that the front door was open, and I instantly got giddy inside.

It wasn't anybody but Shai, and my stalker ass listened intently for his footsteps coming up the stairs. I had his routine down to a science. First, he was going to check on baby Shai, and then he was going to come into our room. His scent reached me before he did. I counted down to one, and he came around the corner looking like a GQ model. His white dress shirt was rolled up to his elbows, and his tie was loosely hanging around his neck. I licked my lips like a horny old lady and tried not to moan at just the sight of him.

He quickly crossed the room, and I raised my head to meet his lips. When he tried to move away, I grabbed his tie and held him there, giving him three more kisses and making him grin.

"You missed me, love?" he asked when I finally let him up for air.

"I always miss you." I simpered.

"That's Sevyn and Zaakir?" He pointed at my phone, where we could still hear them yelling, and I laughed.

"Yep."

"What they arguing about today?"

"Quintuplets." I shrugged like I wasn't the reason behind the whole spat.

He was on his way into his closet but quickly backpedaled with his forehead bunched. "The fuck they arguing about that for?"

"It's a long story," I dismissed, hanging up and sliding my phone under my pillow. My hubby was home, and I was trying to give him all my attention.

Satisfied with my vague ass response, he ducked back into the closet and came out in only his boxers.

"You lookin' at me like you want some Quints." He tilted his head, giving me a look I could feel in my clit.

"Maybe," I teased with a smirk.

"Oh, yeah? Come get in the shower with me." He barely had the request out, and I was already crawling across the bed, stripping out of my gown as I went. I stopped before him, completely naked except for my panties, and he pulled me closer. "We gon' fuck around and not make it to the shower, love." He groaned, cupping my ass in his hands.

"That's cool, too." I was definitely down for whatever he wanted.

With my arms around his neck, he lifted me up, and our lips locked as he carried me into the shower before setting me on my feet. Turning the water on, he moved down my body, sliding my panties down as he went. When I stepped out of them, he quickly had me back in the air with my back against the cool tile.

"I love you, Zuri Miller, soon to be A'santi," he said as he slid inside me, taking my breath away.

"I love you too, Shai A'santi," I managed to get out before he sent me into bliss.

EPILOGUE
ONE YEAR LATER

I stood at the entrance to our reception venue and almost ruined my makeup for the second time that day. To my right stood Zaakir, holding our son, who was only a few months old, in one arm while he held my hand tightly with his other. I'd never in my life felt love so strong as when I looked at them, and I couldn't wait to do forever with him. He shot me his signature panty wetting smile, and I melted inside as the DJ announced us and the double doors opened.

Immediately the beginning of "My Nigga" by YG started to play, and we did our dance inside, rapping to each other as the crowd went crazy. The song fit us perfectly because he was my best friend, and I was his. When I first told Zuri and Ms. Zora that's what we were walking in to, they laughed before admitting that it was definitely the right song for us. They didn't know that it was much deeper than our crazy connection. Zaakir had made sure I was able to get some semblance of peace after the whole thing with Rome. As soon as I was well enough, he took me to where they were holding him so I could witness Rome taking his last breath, putting an end to that chapter of my life. And today, I was entering a new one.

Zaakir handed off Lil Z and met me in the middle of the dance floor for our first dance. I lost my battle with the tears as "ICU" by Coco Jones started to play. Like a best friend should, he knew that was my favorite song, and I melted in his arms.

"You ready to do forever, Mrs. A'santi?" he asked as he spun me around on the dance floor like he'd been doing ballroom all his life. I felt like a straight princess, dress and all, and my prince was dancing me off into the sunset.

"Baby, I been ready. What about you?" I smirked, already knowing that something crazy was about to come out of his mouth from the way his eyes gleamed.

"Shiiiit, I been ready since I realized yo' ass was humming that One Night Only song from Dreamgirls in the elevator that first night," he surprised me by saying and cracked up. That had been my theme song that night, but who would've known our love was going to last much longer than one night? I damn sure didn't. "Yeah, you thought I didn't know! We locked in now, girl. Ain't no breaking up! You good with that?"

"I'm locked all the way in," I promised.

"Even if we have quintuplets?" he teased, making me laugh again, and I pressed a glossy kiss to his lips.

"Anything for you, baby."

ZURI

I watched Sevyn and Zaakir dance and had to wipe my eyes. I'd been crying the whole day because I was so happy for my friend. They'd followed in our footsteps and were married with a baby, just like I said, even though it would've been funnier if she would've had five in one.

"Let's dance, love." Shai appeared at my side and took my hand.

I looked around for SJ and saw him in my mama's lap, talking baby talk to Casa over her shoulder. They stayed going at it because SJ never wanted to share his grandma, and Casa never wanted to share his woman. The fact that my father wasn't there didn't even hurt me like I thought it would. After Kendra finally recovered from the accident, she'd gone straight to jail for what she'd done to Shai's restaurant and for vehicular manslaughter. Apparently, she'd gotten into a collision with an older couple before she got to Suave. The husband died at the scene, and the wife died later at the hospital.

My father blamed Shai for her craziness as usual and hadn't spoken to me since she was sentenced to twenty years. I couldn't lie; at first, I was extremely hurt, and it took some time for me to come to grips with my father turning his back on me for his other child. He was just as toxic as she was, though, and had tried to hide it behind his pro-blackness. I didn't want that energy around me and my family anyway. Honestly, we were better off without him, and his presence wasn't missed at all.

Following Shai out onto the dancefloor, I wasn't surprised that his ass was just as smooth dancing as he was with everything else. He wrapped his arm around my waist and swayed, making me feel butterflies from the way he was looking at me, even with the added weight of our daughter separating us.

I found out I was pregnant again not too long after Sevyn, and I was super excited, especially since it was going to be a girl. All this time, I thought something was wrong with me because I couldn't ever carry to term, and it turned out that it had everything to do with God's timing and the way I was being loved. Shai taught me every day how much he loved me, and I hadn't ever been so happy. My eyebrows shot up in surprise when he spun me around and dipped me like we were in an old movie. That was the reason I was pregnant again already.

I'd had a hard time with love for as long as I could remember, but being with Shai made that all seem like a distant memory from somebody else's life. I was living out my fairytale, and who would've thought that one night alone in Miami would turn into forever?

The End.

ALSO BY J. DOMINIQUE

Alone In Miami At 3AM 2

Alone In Miami At 3Am

First Come Thugs, Then Come Marriage 4

First Come Thugs, Then Come Marriage 3

First Come Thugs, Then Come Marriage 2

First Come Thugs, Then Come Marriage

I Bought Every Dream He Sold Me 3

I Bought Every Dream He Sold Me 2

I Bought Every Dream He Sold Me

In Thug Love With A Chi-Town Millionaire 3

In Thug Love With A Chi-Town Millionaire 2

In Thug Love With A Chi-Town Millionaire

Every Savage Deserves A Hood Chick 2

Every Savage Deserves A Hood Chick

Chino And Chanelle

Chino And Chanelle 2

Chino And Chanelle 3

Giving My Heart To A Chi-Town Menace

Giving My Heart To A Chi-Town Menace: Real & Nova Story

Low Key Fallin' For A Savage

Low Key Fallin' For A Savage 2

Low Key Fallin' For A Savage 3

A Hood Love So Real

A Hood Love So Real 2

The Coldest Savage Stole My Heart

The Coldest Savage Stole My Heart 2

Made in the USA
Columbia, SC
27 March 2025